Pippin Pearmain has traded her placid existence in Lemonwood Cottage for a flurry of activity. There's a ballet to demonstrate, and a crowded visit to Sydney where she makes an agreement with a man who can turn into a dog. She facilitates a proposal and fossicks on the beach for a special gift for her oldest friend. Her newest friend is on the horizon, and a book from the past will soon be making a comeback.

The decade-long lull in Pip's life ended when she reconnected with her cousins, only to lose Cousin Lupin all over again. Since then, Lupin's legacy continues to bring forth wonders.

Her lack of family still troubles her, but now there is a way to leave a legacy for the future anyway. A return to Delphinium Island brings reunions all over again. Mysteries abound, and some of them will slowly unwind to reveal a story that's been generations in the making.

Pip learns that not every question has a clear answer for now. Maybe that's a good thing. As Pip herself says, everyone should have some magic and mystery in their lives.

Performing Pippin Pearmain 8
Copyright © 2023 Lark Westerly
ISBN: 978-1-4874-3723-7
Cover art by Martine Jardin

Published by eXtasy Books Inc

Look for us online at:
www.eXtasybooks.com

PERFORMING PIPPIN PEARMAIN 8

BY

LARK WESTERLY

DEDICATION

For everyone who has ever been claimed by a dog.

AUTHOR'S NOTE

Fiction and Reality

Major places in the story, such as Tasmania, the city of Sydney and the state of Victoria exist in our reality. So does Bass Strait. The towns of Jellico Bay and Delmsford are made up, as is Delphinium Island. The suburb of Windhill is made up. If it existed, it would be somewhere near North Sydney. The suburb of Glebe is real as is the iconic Sydney Harbour Bridge. Oddly, when I invented Tektite, it was almost ten years since we'd had a puppy in our lives. Then Sir Jester Hugh arrived to delight us . . . I was glad to discover I hadn't forgotten much about how puppies *are*.

The story Pip remembers in Chapter Eleven is called *The Ship of Silence,* from the book *In Love with the Wind and Other Stories.*

Penny, Angel, Anemone and Amice, the women Pip meets in Chapter Five, appear in *One Hundred Roses* and *Amice Proposes by Proxy.*

Pip's story covers a year, taking her from her reclusive cottage in Jellico Bay to her old hometown of Delmsford, to the magical fossmere, on to Sydney and thence to Delphinium Island. The nine books compile into one continuing story, slowly revealing the mystery and magic that has been part of Pip's world all along.

And how did I come to write Pip's story? It all began with a flower show . . . and with a bucket.

The story so far . . .

Book One

Introducing Pippin Pearmain—small, eccentric, determined, sixty-six, and ruled by cats. Until a decade ago, Pip earned her living by playing offbeat roles on stage and screen, but after her mother and her agent died in the same week, parts dried up and she moved to Jellico Bay. During a visit to her old hometown she encountered her cousins, Lupin de Leon and Juniper "Jan" Sharman. They, and Jan's daughter, Clarkia, were the only remaining members of the Laurel-Pearmain-de-Leon family. Over afternoon tea at the Delmsford Flower Show, Pip revealed her long-held secret—her bucket list—a literal list of interesting buckets. In return, her cousins wrote down their secrets.

Home in her cottage with the original cat and the back-up cat, who communicate with her in what she thinks of as Cat-Morse, Pip read the secrets. Jan revealed herself as the novelist Juniper Gin. Lupin's secret was shocking—she had just a few months to live.

After Lupin's passing, Jan met the cats Kittisack and Amberjill and received a bucket Pip had promised her for Lupin's last repose. They discussed the provenance of a family heirloom—two copies of a book called *Grandmother's Sunshine*. Lacking heirs, Pip had once offered her copy to a young friend, whose mother refused to let her accept it. A call from Jan's daughter prompted Jan to dash off, leaving Pip with Lupin's legacy—an envelope and a pottery cat.

Book Two

Pip received a call from Magda Saxer, announcing herself as Pip's new agent and offering a role in a film called *Half-Life of the Lost*. The cats were unexpectedly in favour. They suggested Jan's daughter would come to look after them.

Lupin's envelope contained a voucher written in disappearing ink. Pip called the information line, whereupon Gerry Trip, Lupin's ex-colleague at Vouch-Safe, informed her she had one hour to prepare for a mystery Experience.

Gerry's step-grandson, Jamie, promised to cat-sit. He drove Pip to a rendezvous.

Pip boarded the yacht *Tulpenmanie*, crewed by pleasant Zach, his odd girlfriend, Jisinia, and Jamie's uncle, Tane.

When Pip realised Tane was missing, she called triple zero. Jisinia confiscated the phone but returned it. Pip rationalised that Tane must have returned to shore.

That night, Tane, who was a silversmith, came back. After resizing a ring for her, he invited Pip to meet his family. She agreed.

Tane picked her up and jumped into the sea.

Book Three

Tane took Pip through an underwater gateway to *over there* where she spent a week with his extended family, practising ballet with Jane and making friends with Tane's spouse, Jillian Jules. The fossmere, a waterfall pool, delighted Pip. She left her tektite ring in the cave behind the falls in gratitude for her adventure. Tane and Jules took her to Hob's Island where she added a new bucket to her list. A sighting of dolphins gave her the idea for a ballet.

Back at Lemonwood Cottage, Pip discovered Jamie, her driver, was a mutie or *mutable fay*. He had a second self—a dog he called Kakao.

Jan asked if her daughter Clarkia might come to stay at Lemonwood Cottage while Pip had her screen test.

Book Four

Pip met her agent, Magda, at Sydney airport. Magda's friend, Pandora, drove them to a guesthouse run by Edgar and Joan Treadwell. Next morning, Edgar took Pip to a grassy area *over there* to do her ballet practice.

Pip went with Magda to Diamond Spellman Studio for a screen test where she met the film crew . . . and also Matin Campania, from Arts in Tune, the company co-producing the film.

The filming was to be part of a dance festival. Pip looked forward to researching music for her dolphin ballet.

On the way back from the screen test, Pip visited the Fairy Gardens, where she saw sculpted statues of the founders. She decided to commission the sculptor to make her a bucket. He was away, so Pip left a message with the alarming Frances le Fay.

Pip borrowed an encyclopaedia called *Orders of the Fay* from Edgar and also ordered a set from Jonquil Orange of The Orange Grove bookshop. On a whim, she enquired about *Grandmother's Sunshine*. Jonquil believed it was a myth but said someone else had asked for it recently. Pip prevaricated, unwilling to admit her family had two copies of such a rare title.

After a return to the fossmere to dance with Jane and work on her dolphin ballet, *Delphine,* Pip went to the Fairy Gardens to finish blocking the ballet. There, she met the Dames with Dogs. Her attempt to use Cat-Morse on the dogs failed. She spotted a mutie . . . a young man with a Scottie dog self. She tried Dog-Morse on an uncooperative black spaniel who was revealed to be Gillan, the mutie's mother. From her time at the fossmere, Pip identified Gillan and her sons as piskies.

Gillan recognised Pip from her role in the cult film *The House of Heriot,* in which she had starred with Alain Barfleur. Finding Gillan hard work, Pip left, but Gillan made her a remarkable offer.

Book Five

Pip tried and failed to take herself *over there* without a pilot. She then travelled to Delphinium Island with Magda in Matin Campania's van. Magda asked for details about *Grandmother's Sunshine*. Matin distracted her, to Pip's relief.

At the island, they met Gillan's son Mull St Ives. Pip and Magda were assigned a cabin. Pip went to the Icehouse market for an official shirt, where she met Jessie and Asher, two elves, and encountered Tane Pendennis from *Tulpenmanie* and the fossmere.

Pip joined other dancers and musicians to Dance in the Dawn, and saw Matin's wife, Tamzin Campania, playing her fiddle. She did ballet practice with Tane's daughter Jane, who had arrived with her cousin, Jamie's sister Laura. Jane had found principal dancers for Pip's ballet.

Pip met Costas Capricorn who played impromptu music for her ballet rehearsal.

Filming began for *Half-Life of the Lost*. Pip met the actors, members of a company called Biblio-Rep, the crew from Diamond Spellman Studio, eccentric wardrobe master, Ward, and Humphry "Humph" Carpenter-Rivers, the playwright, who had invented a new prologue for two people and a horse.

With the prologue in the can, Pip filmed the first scene with Star Calder-Quince, who played comatose Perdita.

During the break, Pip headed to the barn where she met Tamzin again. She was started to see the drawing Tamzin was working on . . . a copy of a picture in *Grandmother's Sunshine*.

Pip learned that she and Tamzin had known one another twenty-five years before. Tamzin had been her little friend, Angie Blake, who had lived for a while in Pip's hometown in Tasmania. They arranged to meet the next morning to discuss ballet music . . . and Pip hatched a new plan.

Book Six

Pip put her plan for the family heirloom, *Grandmother's Sunshine,* to her cousins, and received a cautious go-ahead on her suggestion that they might have copies made to share. She also talked to the cats about the possibility of bringing home a fay puppy to live at Lemonwood Cottage. To her surprise, the cats were in favour. Pip decided to call her puppy *Tektite*.

Working hard on her role as Solace in *Half-Life of the Lost,* Pip still found time to attend a rehearsal of her ballet, *Delphine*. She was thrilled at the way it was shaping under the capable work of the Forever troupe, but a wee bit sad that it was now out of her hands. Since her friend Jane was also unable to have much to do with *Delphine,* Pip decided to work on her little cat ballet, *Queen of the Clowder.* Jane came up with a way to fit it into Pip's already crammed schedule. Star Calder-Quince joined the enterprise, and she and Pip grew closer. They were so engrossed in conversation that they almost missed a filming call — twice. Pip's agent, Magda, was angry, and Pip promised to do better.

Star's daughter Candlemas asked to join the cat ballet. Star confided to Pip that the Caraway's Comforts brand of skincare was in fact her family's business. Pip wanted to know more, but Star couldn't tell her. It was time they were both onstage.

Book Seven

Pip told Magda and Tamzin the plan for *Grandmother's Sunshine.*

Pip and her band of amateurs presented *Queen of the Clowder* and were invited to demonstrate it at the Forever studio after the festival.

Delphine premiered.

The last scene of *Half-Life of the Lost* was filmed, but Humph had changed the script. He announced a new epilogue, in which the horseman from the prologue would spirit Solace away. Pip was shocked to recognise the new horseman as her old friend Alain Barfleur. Pip and Alain had supper together, but their reunion was interrupted by Tamzin and Matin.

Pip returned home. Clarkia decided to stay on at the cottage. Jan arranged publication of *Grandmother's Sunshine* with her publishers. Star made a flying visit to carry out a scheme she and Pip had hatched, helping Pip to keep a promise to her late mother.

Book Eight, the one you're about to read, brings more surprises for Pip in a visit to Sydney, a return home, and a meeting with some most unusual dogs.

The story continues . . .

CHAPTER ONE. INTERIM

Jan came to stay at Lemonwood Cottage for a few days with Pip and Clarkia midway through June. That suited Pip because her cousin agreed to take her to the airport.

"It'll give me a chance to check out sewing shops in the city," as Jan put it.

Pip hadn't realised Jan was interested in sewing, but now she saw it should have been obvious. All that applique of lavender and leaping beagles on pinafore bibs and shirts must be Jan's own work. It seemed a wee bit surprising. Little Nanna Pearmain had been an expert embroiderer, but she was no relation to Jan.

Pip hoped Jan would enjoy her festival shirt when they went to *Tales in Tune* in July. Maybe she'd want to do her own embroidery.

Magda Saxer, Pip's agent, had called two days after Star's flying visit to inform Pip that the *Forever* gig was going ahead on the seventeenth of June, and would she please note down the booking details for her flight.

"And while you're in the mood, there's been a request for you to appear in a little documentary called *Amateur Acclaim*. There's a decent appearance fee, and it seems to be a classy production."

"Where would I have to go?" Pip asked. Until recently, she'd hardly left Jellico Bay in a decade. After the excitement of the festival, film, and ballet on Delphinium Island, she'd settled back into the cottage to embark on her first adventure with decoupage.

"They come to you—the idea is filming their subjects in their home environments. The crew will be at the *Forever* gig, so you can meet them informally before you decide."

Pip spun the ring of kindness, which she had taken to wearing on her left ring finger back in April. Clarkia had probably noticed it, but she hadn't commented.

That was the upside of being a card-carrying eccentric, Pip thought. One could wear a ring made from braided hair and no one would consider it odd. Well, no odder than all the other things one did.

"Thanks," she said into the phone. "I'll do that."

"I understand why you might hesitate," Magda said.

"You mean because it could so easily be an indulgent piece showcasing a quaint little woman who is a life-long amateur dancer."

"Exactly." Magda sounded grimly amused. "The term *quirky* might well come into play, more than once, as well."

"One *quirk* or even the suspicion of a *cute* and the answer is *no*. Doubly so if anyone misuses *unique* or calls me a reclusive star."

"What are your feelings regarding the term *ingenue*?" Magda sounded genuinely curious.

"I'd have to be young and endearingly innocent to be one of those again."

"So you were one, once? I wondered."

"Yes. *Petite wide-eyed ingenue*, I was called. Then I became *diminutive, offbeat character actress*."

"How odd, to be defined by newspaper reviews."

"Tell me about it," Pip said.

"So, *Amateur Acclaim*. It's your call."

Pip heard a faint expensive *clink* as Magda put down her crystal whiskey glass.

Pip rarely drank alcohol, but her first agent, Sully, who had died suddenly in 2012, had downed copious drafts of Fagus

Ale without obvious ill effects.

"If you're going to drink, drink the best you can afford," had been one of Sully's favoured maxims. "That way you won't overdo it, and you won't be drinking rotgut."

Magda, who had been Sully's friend and who had lately taken up the role as Pip's agent, enjoyed a dram of Tom Cat Hill single malt, an exclusive whiskey from a boutique distillery. She generally drank it from the *kiss* glass her husband had given her as a token of his devotion.

Pip had her own *kiss* cup, decorated with marigolds. It had been a gift to her fifty years before from a young man with whom she'd worked on the film *The House of Heriot.* She had loved that cup for decades, but until she met Alain Barfleur again at the *Dance in Tune* festival, she'd had no idea what it represented. It was a *kiss of kindness,* Alain had explained. That made it somewhat different from the glass Magda had, which was a *kiss of married love.*

There were enormous numbers of things Pip had not known until recently. If she hadn't had a horror of buzz-terms and jargon, she might have said her learning curve was steeper than the sides of Mount O'Connor.

Magda added, "I wasn't going to come to hold your hand when you do the *Forever* gig, since you organised it for yourself. But then I thought I could come anyway. I can so easily use the pixie forest gate. It debouches in a copse just a few minutes' walk from *Forever.*"

"Oh." Pip knew she probably sounded noncommittal. In her mind it was more like, *Oh! Oh! Oho!*

Pip restrained herself from dancing a jig of joy. Magda had mentioned that gateway before, but she hadn't put the connotations together in her mind.

If I can find a pilot, I can go to the fossmere. No jumping in the sea and clambering up a rocky path. Just step through from a green-belt into a magical forest.

The thoughts clinked together like interlocking rings.

3

Jane's coming to the gig to reprise her role as Princess Hopeful. I can go to the fossmere with her when she goes home.

She thanked Magda, said sedately that she looked forward to seeing her at the *Forever* Studio, and ended the call.

She resumed her cautious application of glue to the wooden jar which was her first venture into decoupage.

Clarkia, shredding red cabbage for one of her inventive soups, stilled her knife and looked up. "You seem awfully pleased with yourself, Pip. As pleased as Mum seemed when Dad finally admitted that riding a high-powered motorbike was not in his best interests and traded it for a bush-basher. Mind, she didn't nag him. There would have been no point. Sometimes people have to realise things on their own."

So that, Pip thought, solved the tiny mystery of Jan's unexpected bounciness when they'd spoken on the phone a while ago.

"Good news?" Clarkia asked, setting her knife back in motion.

Until recently, Pip's kitchen had been deficient in all sorts of things—she hadn't even had kitchen scissors—but since Clarkia came to stay the kitchenware situation had miraculously improved.

"You could say that," Pip said, choosing an orange tulip cut-out to apply. "Nothing about motorbikes, though." She added, casually, "I'll be away a bit longer than I thought when I do the amateur ballet gig. Are you okay with the cats for ten days or so?"

"Fine. And I'll keep working on the goat ballet story and do my practice."

"Perfect." Pip had become fond of Clarkia. She wasn't bright and colourful, full of presence, and *fervent* the way Tamzin Campania, Candlemas Calder-Quince, and Jane Pendennis were. She was more like Jane's cousin Laura and, indeed, like Jane's sister Sulane. Clarkia was' a calm, friendly, *practical* young woman who had suffered a nasty betrayal but who wasn't — what was the modern term? Aha! Wasn't letting it define her.

Clarkia was a good person. Pip liked her for much more than their blood connection.

Recently, Clarkia had started doing basic ballet with Pip, so the two of them shared morning practice. They didn't share Pip's eight o'clock ritual of lemon juice from the evil-minded lemon tree in the garden mixed with hot water because Clarkia, having tasted it once, pulled a disgusted face and told Pip she'd stick to her favourite cinnamon mocha.

Like Jan, she also had no love for Pip's camomile or cambric tea, but she did share Pip's enjoyment of tarts from the Queen of Tarts range. She brought their shared order home from *Jelly-and-Juice* every Friday after her shift. She did some light gardening, went out with local friends, helped unpack the boxes and crates, and generally got on with life.

Pip thought she made an excellent housemate, being available but not pervasive, allowing Pip as much space as she needed to be her usual self.

Almost her usual self, anyway. The usual self she'd been at the beginning of the year had not wanted company, and she had *not* been plotting to hitch a ride to fairyland.

Pip had told Jan about the *Dance in Tune* festival and the filming of *Half-Life of the Lost*. She told her of meeting Magda and rediscovering an old friend in Tamzin Campania and described the ballet. She thought Jan hadn't really understood. Probably no one would who hadn't been there. Pip wasn't sure that she understood herself. She hoped the magic camaraderie of creating *Queen of the Clowder* would revive in a different venue, but she knew there were no guarantees.

She smoothed the tulip scrap and tried to peel her thumb free without leaving prints. "Bother! If I'd known it was going to be this complicated, I'd never have started it," she sulked.

"Ja. *Und?*" Clarkia bundled cabbage into the pot. "Want

some help from Mum or me, or would you rather inter the evidence in the compost and pretend it never happened?"

"I'm thinking," Pip said with dignity. Then she raised her chin. "I'm going to get this done. Then I can start on my bucket."

Jan, who had been watching with amusement, put aside her sewing and came to inspect the jar. "I think you've got too much glue."

"I know, but when I used less it wouldn't stick."

Chapter Two. B&B

Jan drove Pip to the airport, and she flew to Melbourne. This time, she held her peace regarding the cabin staff's appalling tea-making regime, which she noted had not improved despite her previous lecture. She'd chosen to bring a flask of camomile tea made to her own requirements and occupied herself by rubbing dried glue out of her shirt. She must have brushed against her practice piece on the way out the door. She hoped the piece would be dry by the time she returned, but she wasn't banking on it.

Thinking back over its impressive undulations, she admitted silently that maybe it wouldn't ever take its place on the mantelpiece next to Lupin's Cat and Little Pop's brass candlesticks, *or* on the hall table near Little Nanna Pearmain's river-and-ducks embroidery.

Pippin Pearmain is inept at decoupage.

She pulled herself together. It was her first attempt. Did artists hang their first attempts in galleries? Did vocalists get a Number One after a single singing lesson? Did dancers perform principal roles after practising for fifty-eight years?

Well yes — sometimes.

She was living proof of that.

Pip smiled and began to hum.

Two people in the row ahead rubbed their necks and shivered.

Pip met Star and Candlemas Calder-Quince and Humph Carpenter-Rivers at the airport. Star and Candlemas lit up in welcome and Humph asked, *sotto voce*, if he knew the lady in green, and, if so, was she Pippin Pearmain, whom they'd planned to meet.

Reassured on that point, he beamed at Pip and shook her hand as if she was a long-lost friend returned to the fold. His quiff was as insouciant as ever, and he had on an extravagant cravat Pip hadn't seen before, fastened with his usual gold pin.

"Do I know him?" he asked, gazing past Pip's ear.

Pip turned and saw a man of about forty wearing a cap and carrying a hold-all. He was looking around, somewhat bemused.

Star, glancing the same way, stuck two fingers in her mouth and whistled shrilly. "Boots! Over here!"

Grant Chapman, who usually danced with *Dad Ballet*, but who had joined *Queen of the Clowder* as Puss in Boots, closed the gap between them in a series of pirouettes.

"Ham," Star muttered.

"I do know him, even without his ears and tail," Humph concluded. "Hi, Boots."

Grant tipped his hat. "Back at ya, Dappercat." He turned to Star and Candlemas. "Slinky Twinkle and Downtrodden Tabby. And—" He swivelled and made a grand reverence to Pip. "Our beloved Reigna La Chatte, Queen of the Clowder." He looked left and right. "Anyone else here?"

"Not as far as I know," Star said. "The others are all more local, I think. Except for Jane. Not sure where she's from."

Pip knew very well where Jane Pendennis was from, but she didn't feel it was her place to explain.

As planned, the stately Flori Almaclair met them at the car park and drove them to Patterdale, where she deposited them at the prebooked *Over Here B&B*.

This turned out to be a large house inhabited by a pretty calico cat that reminded Pip of Amberjill, a flock of peculiar geese loitering near the steps, and a quiet, handsome man who introduced himself as Kris Peckerdale, father of Corin and Jisinia.

"You know Corin from your dolphin ballet, of course," he said to Pip. "And Jisinia informs me you spent an interesting time with her aboard *Tulpenmanie.*"

It was a shock for Pip to realise Corin, who danced the sea-fay man in *Delphine,* was the brother of Zach Rowan's odd girlfriend who had flimflammed her phone during her V-S Experience. At least that explained the similarity of their bi-coloured eyes. She had noted that without realising what it meant. Heterochromia wasn't very common, and yet she'd met two people displaying it within a couple of weeks.

Belatedly, Pip realised the calico cat, which also had different-coloured eyes, making *three* instances of that phenomenon, must be the *Mistress Calico* Jisinia had mentioned to her aboard the yacht. That was back in April, but it seemed a long time ago. She had packed more new activity into the few weeks since then than she'd managed in the whole preceding decade.

She smiled vaguely at Kris Peckerdale and said she did indeed know his children. She couldn't help thinking of Magda's friend Pandora Inkersoll, who was Kris' half-sister, and who had begged the heavens to save her from her niece Jisinia. Jin was clearly an acquired taste.

The B&B, Kris warned them all, had a horribly unreliable Wi-Fi connection and almost no phone service.

Apart from that, Pip found it delightful and full of character, with the rooms painted with magical murals and trompe l'oeil.

There was even a bucket to add her list, an old-fashioned, wide-mouthed milk bucket, painted with a finely detailed garden scene and holding a pot of winter roses that reminded her of Aunt Helen. The botanical name of the winter rose was *hellebore,* and Aunt Helen had been officially named Hellebore Rose. Hellebore's twin, Rose Guelder, had been Pip's own Little Mum. Botanical names were a feature in their family. Pip occasionally entertained herself with a wistful list of names she might have given a child if she'd ever had one.

With Cousin Lupin gone to glory, and Cousin Juniper "Jan" at sixty-four just two years younger than Pip, it would be left to Jan's daughter Clarkia to carry on the family . . . if she chose. And Pip was completely aware it *was* Clarkia's choice.

And if she does choose, she'll have to stop hanging out with exclusively female friends.

Not that Pip blamed her younger cousin for being unenthusiastic regarding men. Her partner of four years had betrayed her by a double-life scam that lasted until the other woman got tired of it and confronted the blameless Clarkia with evidence of his duplicity. Pip generally enjoyed a good scheme, but she didn't approve of whatever-his-name's activities.

Pip sat cross-legged on the single bed in the attic of the B&B, which she had chosen from the available rooms. Humph and Grant were on the ground floor, possibly working up a bit more business between their ballet characters. Star and her daughter had taken a twin room on the second floor. Pip had headed for the highest available perch.

Her temporary eyrie was small and compact. It had a miniature fig tree growing on the balcony, and although it wasn't fruiting at present, it added a lovely Mediterranean touch to the place. There was a tea and coffee nook with fine china painted with more winter roses. Pip wished she'd brought her marigold kiss cup so she could sit in lovely surroundings and think of Alain. He'd said the cup let him know if she was happy, but maybe the ring of kindness would do as well.

She had an urge to call him, to arrange a visit to his manor on Flaxen Isle as he had suggested, but that was impossible.

Over there was a literal step away when one was in the right place, but as far as phones were concerned, it might as well be at the bottom of the Mariana Trench.

Or maybe phones do work in the Mariana Trench. What do I know?

Sometimes, the depth of her ignorance of such matters surprised her.

She couldn't call Alain, but there *was* a way to get in touch with him, maybe in July. To do that, she planned to make the acquaintance of two scary people. Mariner van der Strand would take a message to Alain. His wife, Meri, would make sure he did it properly. Or so Pip had heard. She hadn't met either of them yet. If they were anything like the seafay man she'd seen when she first visited *over there* in the company of Tane Pendennis, they would probably be scarier than anyone else she'd met—even her agent Magda in a strop.

Are you a woman or a wimp?

Unfortunately, the answer was an unequivocal *both*.

CHAPTER THREE FOREVER

The Forever Studio was the place where Pip and her temporary troupe were to demonstrate *Queen of the Clowder* to the raw recruits of the dancing school. It was situated in a large seven-storey complex called the Peckerdale Grene Tower, a short drive from the B&B.

Pip met Magda there by arrangement. Her agent had come through the gate the day before and was staying with her old friends Pia and Peter P. Magda lived in Western Australia, but by courtesy of her small amount of fay blood and by the good offices of her full fay husband and their daughters, she was able to use the gateways to-and-from *over there* to make a quick transit that would otherwise take hours in a long flight between capital cities.

When Pip enquired, it turned out that Marianna Mackenzie had done the honours.

Daughters were such useful things, Pip considered. She did wish she'd thought to have one.

"I'm not here as your agent this time," Magda reiterated gruffly. "Just taking a chance to catch up as friends."

It startled Pip to think of the formidable Magda Quest Saxer as a friend. She hadn't known her long. Her original agent, Sullivan "Sully" Gilbert, had been with her since childhood and when she'd passed on a decade before, Pip had been bereft.

Sully hadn't been a friend, exactly, though — more like a cross between a kindly aunt and a no-nonsense fairy godmother who waved her wand and commanded things to happen.

In contrast, Pip had spent less than a fortnight with Magda, although they'd spoken a few times on the phone. She'd also suffered a right bollocking — well-deserved — from her agent when she'd got talking to Star and almost been late for a scene in *Half-Life of the Lost*. That would have been a professional disaster, as both she and Star were present in every scene but the prologue.

Bollocking aside, two weeks was not enough time to form a friendship.

And now you're being ridiculous. You've known Star even less time, and she is definitely your friend. And Alain . . .

She'd spent three weeks with Alain Barfleur back when she was sixteen, and that had been enough for her to remember him fondly for half a century.

"Good to see you," she said to Magda.

Actually, it was. Magda wasn't Sully, but the two women had known one another for years, and it was down to Magda that Pip was here at the *Forever* studio. She owed Magda a lot.

The rest of the troupe assembled without fuss. Laura Pendennis, her young aunt Amaryllis Trip, and the two Merriweather brothers who danced the tommies' roles in the ballet must have all lived nearby, because they arrived to greet Pip and the others shortly after they came from the B&B. Jane Pendennis dead heated with them, emerging from a copse of English trees and running across the greensward to embrace Pip, Star, and Candlemas with enthusiasm that almost knocked Pip down.

Everyone seemed eager to get back into tails and ears and dance their small solos. As for Pip, she slid back into the role of the old queen as if she'd never been away.

The demonstrations of *Queen of the Clowder* were intensive, with the raw *new intake,* as Flori had termed them, visibly awed at the idea of being able to dance in an actual ballet *soon.* Pip's troupe ranged in age from fifteen-year-old Candlemas to Humph, who must be well over seventy. It encompassed the tall Laura, Tango and Tempo, the moderate Star, Grant, Candlemas, and Jane and the decidedly small Amaryllis, Pip, and Humph. Grant was a semi-pro with *Dad Ballet* and Pip was a perpetual amateur. Even Allirra Diamond, who was not a dancer at all, had turned up to reprise her cameo role as Scary Houndie. With all these contrasting performers, it was no wonder the *Forever* recruits soon lost their inhibitions.

The film crew for the *Amateur Acclaim* documentary was there for some of the time and, far from being patronising and pushy, the young filmmakers seemed genuinely devoted to finding what made true amateurs tick, especially, as one of them put it, when a person was professional in one field and amateur in a related one.

Pip turned them over to Magda to make the terms for her appearance and threw herself into dancing her beloved cat queen in her ballet.

Delphine was a triumph, and she would always love it, but *Queen of the Clowder* was *hers*. It celebrated amateurs and a range of talents, ages, and body shapes, and it let her play to her strength in ad-libbing, as the queen responded to gains and errors made by her clowder.

If it had been possible, Pip would have hugged the queen and invited her to visit Lemonwood Cottage to schmooze with Kittisack, Amberjill, and Lupin's cat.

That was ridiculous, of course.

Or not. If I have a pottery cat guardian which communicates in Cat-Morse, why not a virtual queen cat to hug?

There was a slight awkwardness when Star and Humph supposed Pip would be returning to the airport with them, Grant, and Allirra in Flori Almaclair's van.

She was trying to train herself out of prevarication, and especially out of fibs-of-expedience-or-convenience, but what could she do? Star and the others were human, and as far as Pip knew they had no idea there was anything else to be. Star already thought she was daft, and liked her for it, but if she started talking of fairyland ... well! She *could* explain properly, but she had the gut feeling *disclosure* was meant to be done by someone with fay blood, not by random people who had fallen in with fairies. Magda had explained all that to her, but she didn't want to annoy her trace-fay agent by asking her to explain it again to Star and Candlemas and Humph.

Fortunately, before she got herself wound up in a mess of evasions, a very tall woman with a long face turned up at the guesthouse and asked to see Pippin Pearmain.

Pip stared at her for a few seconds in half-recognition.

"Sam Silver," the woman said, holding out a long-fingered hand. "I met you at the fossmere."

"Of course! Jules' daughter. I looked out for you and your family at the festival, but Tane said you'd gone to the tower instead."

"That's right," Sam said easily. She added, "Jane is staying on with Laura and Cade for tonight, and she asked me if I could pilot you to the fossmere. She'll meet you there in a day or so, and she says Ardal will be waiting to take you riding and Trae will play for your practice. Does that make sense?"

"Perfect sense," Pip said. "I'll just tell the others I've met a local friend and I'm having dinner with her family."

Sam looked amused. "You do that, Miss Pearmain. Dinner it is, but I'm sure everyone will want you to stay longer. You fit in so well with the madhouse at the foss."

"Implying I'm mad as well," Pip said dryly.

Sam laughed. "You have to be to survive *chez Tane and Jillian Jules.* I do love them, though—especially Tally."

"Why especially Tally?" Pip questioned. Tallien was the youngest of Tane and Jillian's brood—a loud and demanding baby boy with cyclonic lungs.

Sam grinned. "Think of him and think of our Soash."

"Oh. Right. Mind you, Soash is older."

"Yes, but she never was as loud as Tally. Not loud at all. She takes after my darling Oash who is the sweetest thing on legs." Sam went into a bit of a reverie, evidently reflecting upon her partner . . . or spouse. Pip wasn't sure which. She was also unsure of the pronouns to use. Oash was a pureblood sylvan, and with that order gender was a matter of choice.

Sam said, "I warn you, Soash and Mirri will want you to dance with them again, and Oash will probably ply you with apricot jam. We made a huge boiling of it, and we have jars and jars and *jars*. Oash has a most peculiar relationship with apricot jam, and a proper horror of ever running out. I expect you're tough enough to weather the jam, and Tane, and Tally, and that bumptious pony, and everything else the fossmere can throw at you—right?"

Pip nodded mendaciously. She had never considered herself bold, brave, or tough in any degree, but she admired Sam and she didn't want to disappoint her.

Sam beamed at her as if at a child who had performed exceptionally well in a difficult test. "When you're ready to go home, one of us can bring you back here, or else you could get Ardal to take you to the castle bridge gate and fly home from Sydney."

Pip found it weird that the very odd Sam Silver knew about flights and timetables, but then, hadn't someone said she'd lived as a human until she met Oash? She was at least partly human, which Oash wasn't.

Pip didn't ask for the details, but she thanked Sam and said she'd consider it.

I'm going to the fossmere . . . She danced a few steps with delight.

She'd had a fine time at *Forever*, but her mind was already leaping ahead to the people and places she'd come to love.

How lucky am I? I'm having a holiday in fairyland.

She smiled, as Kittisack's voice sounded silently in her head. *Tell no one.*

CHAPTER FOUR. TROLLIE

Pip spent a week at the fossmere, dancing with Jane and the little girls, foraging with Sulane, sitting in the pools with Mama Tam and Jillian, and riding the chalklands with Ardal Cornfellow.

Even little Tally's roars seemed to be waning in frequency and volume as he gained a bit more maturity. He had developed a delightful gummy grin which he bestowed on Pip every morning. She sometimes fetched him from his cradle when he woke and carried him to Jillian to be fed.

Might as well get in the swing of the needs of little young things before I meet the puppy.

After her conversation with Tane at the festival she felt a bit uneasy for the hob lad's happiness. She knew he was devoted to Jane, and that Jane was flexing her wings and working out her future, planning a visit to her partly-human grandmother and scheming to join the *Forever* troupe as soon as she deemed herself skilled enough. Ardal, potter and horse trainer who almost never strayed from his homely surroundings, must be wondering if there was a place for him in that future, but he seemed as placid and cheerful as ever to Pip.

He and Jane were very young, but Pip understood the fay often paired up as soon as they had, in their terms, *enough years*. This habit, or tradition, or whatever it was, led to some impressively long partnerships almost unmatched in the human realm. Magda's old friends at the tower, Pia and Peter P, had been together for more than seventy years and had accrued more than a dozen descendants. Pip knew at least five of them.

She elected to return to Jellico Bay via Sydney rather than go back to the Melbourne airport from the tower. She wanted to call on the Treadwells and visit the Fairy Gardens again and possibly to harass Frances le Fay about the bucket. *Surely* the woodcarver called Xavier whose phone Frances was babysitting had got off the galleon by now! If not, he ought to, Pip thought. He had a bucket to make.

Not getting any younger here.

Frances had promised to pass on Pip's message, but she'd sounded altogether flighty and hyper-enthusiastic on the phone, so who knew what might have distracted her from her duty.

On the appointed day, Ardal brought Fimber the pony along to conduct Pip to the castle bridge gateway. Fimber wore what Ardal termed a *glove saddle,* a felt pad with stirrups. The leathers tucked neatly under felt flaps and didn't pinch at all.

"Happen he'll miss you," Ardal said as Pip settled herself in the saddle. Fimber was not tall, and not ill-tempered, but he was wily. Pip appreciated his need to assert himself. Ponies were like small people—often overlooked and underestimated. He reminded her of an equine version of Humph.

"I'll miss him, the villain," she said, stroking Fimber's silver-grey neck and breathing in the agreeable scent of healthy horse.

"Happen we all have folk to miss," Ardal mentioned, as he mounted his own solid bay, Indi. He turned to Pip. "Be a sad thing if not," he added.

Pip consulted her heart, which missed so many people she'd loved or depended upon over the years. It had been a simple equation once. She'd missed folk who'd left her life. In the early days of performing, Little Mum and Sully had gone with her to filming jobs, and Little Dad had come to visit the set if the shoot was a long one.

Nowadays, it was more complicated. She missed her life at the cottage while she was away. That didn't prevent her from longing for the fossmere, or for Delphinium Island, or for places she had never been when she was at home. She wished she could live a parallel life . . . one life at home and the other . . . or others . . . peripateticking — was that a word? — around her other favourite places.

"Maybe you're right," she said.

"I'll take the missing any day over the never loving," Ardal said pensively. "Are you ready, Miss Pip?"

"I'm ready." Pip, clad in the neat and practical riding clothes Sulane had given her on her first visit, touched her heel to Fimber, who responded with a naughty swish of his tail. She did it again and he stepped out, bustling to keep up with Indi's longer stride and implying he could have moved on earlier if his lackadaisical rider had explained properly.

At the castle gate, they encountered Flick Dark carrying one of her baskets from the castle. Ardal flagged her down and handed Pip over to be conducted, so Pip thought regretfully, like someone's left luggage through the gate. Her actual luggage came with her, conjured up from the fossmere by Ardal.

She *quite* understood why the fay sometimes flew under the radar. Who could fail to envy someone who need never turn back ten minutes into a drive because he'd forgotten his phone?

Flick did the transfer nicely, talking of the children she shared with her human husband, the honey she had from her bees, and how much she hoped to have a new child one day soon. She smelled comfortingly of marzipan.

"Another girl, I hope, because our George — ah, here we are — take my hand, or you can hold my elbow if you prefer."

Pip turned to catch a glimpse of Ardal, Fimber, and Indi, and was touched to see the hob lad had waited to wave goodbye.

What a lovely lad he was.

Her mind drifted to another lovely lad she'd known.

Her phone, waking from its fairy-land coma, gave a cheerful *ching* announcing a message from Magda. Pip said a quick but sincere thanks-and-farewell to Flick before she went to tap on the guesthouse door.

Through Sam Silver's good offices, she had booked her old room for the night. She was let in and invited to drink tea and eat parkin with the proprietors, Edgar and Joan.

They felt like old friends, so much so that Pip relaxed into describing the buckets on her list, and the new one she hoped soon to acquire . . . if Xavier Partridge ever got off the galleon.

She assured them that the bucket they'd given her—the one showing a fairyland scene with Edgar and Joan depicted as friendly trolls—was one of the prides of her collection.

To her surprise, the couple exchanged rueful glances, and Edgar bit his lip like a guilty schoolboy.

"What?" she asked, rather sharply.

Joan, a handsome woman who was dressed in neatly tailored trousers and a loose and beautiful winter-weight caftan top, said, to her husband, "Happen we'd better tell the lass, Eddie? Introduce her to Trollie, shall we?"

"Eh, I don't know, Joan." Edgar looked guiltier than ever. "Happen it'll afear t' lass."

Pip frowned. Edgar had told her he'd been born in Merimbula, on the human side of the gates. Despite this, he spoke like a stage Yorkshireman. He and Joan *lived human*, but she was aware they were pureblood hobs. They might not have been related to Ardal Cornfellow or to William Cliff, the other two hobs she knew, but they were of the same order and displayed the same general characteristics. She would have bet on her life there was nothing to fear from hobs. The *Orders of the Fay* books concurred. Hobs were reckoned high among the kindest and most reliable of the major orders. *Plainspoken folk, clear as their cider.*

Joan's hand moved to caress her impressive string of pearls, which she'd told Pip had been a gift from Edgar to celebrate twenty-five years of marriage. It seemed an odd gem for him to have chosen. Pip would have expected rubies. The wedding ring on Joan's finger glowed green with what was probably not an emerald, but some kind of inlay.

"Pippin is not the fearful type, love. Doughty as a hob sow is our Pippin," Joan said.

Pip wondered if that was a compliment. She wanted to argue that no, on the contrary, she was a timorous soul, but something held her back. Maybe, she thought, she was braver than she believed. Wasn't she planning to scrape acquaintance with Mariner and Meri van der Strand as the first step to visiting her old friend Alain? The seafay couple were friends of the Campanias, but Tamzin had implied she was still cautious around them.

Pip had seen one seafay man already. From her brief sighting, she remembered him as — disturbing. Was she really going to ask *two* seafay for a favour? She was. Therefore . . .

Pip held her peace and looked doughty. She didn't even have to try. That was an advantage of being a lifelong performer. "Who is Trollie?"

Joan nodded her appreciation of Pip's directness. "Happen you know a mutie or so, Pippin?"

Pip relaxed. "I know four, and I've seen at least a couple more."

"Aye?" Joan seemed to be waiting for her to expound.

"I know Jamie pretty well. He's a lovely lad who has an extra self who is a dog called Kakao. I also know Gillan, who has a bitch self, and I've met her sons, Zennor and Mull, who have dog selves too. I've seen others in their family. I know Jillian Jules, and a sylvan called Oash who Jules' daughter's love, but I don't know if they count."

"Let's say they do, for the purpose of this exercise," Joan said. "So, you're familiar with the concept of second selves who might look a lot different from what we call the main or primary self."

"You sound like a lecturer," Pip said.

Joan grinned at her. "I am, my lass. University of the third age."

"They love my Joan," Edgar put in. He added thoughtfully, "They also love the cider and parkin."

Pip said, "Okay. I'm familiar with Jillian who is also Jules, and with people who can manifest as dogs. Are you suggesting Edgar has a dog self?"

She pictured the kind of dog Edgar might manifest. Surely a huge and shaggy battledog with the kindliest nature.

"Not a dog," Joan said.

"He is sometimes she?" Pip ventured politely. *A large, hairy she with an impressive bosom. An Amazon.*

Edgar laughed, sounding like stones tumbling in a barrel. "Eh, lass—that I am not."

"Cat?" *A large, hairy tom with a cuddly disposition. Not like that fay beast I met when I was staying here before.*

"Nay!"

"What then? I suppose there are all sorts of mutable forms, but I've met only dogs . . . and folk with sylvan blood. Oh, and one old priest who has a cat self, although I didn't know at the time. That's it . . . as far as I know," she added cautiously, remembering Court Leopold who had played the horseman in the *Half-Life of the Lost*. He had changed into a flamboyant costume for his role but had seemed *so* different he might as well have been another person. Possibly, he was.

Joan smiled. "So, you know our friend Gillan. Without going into too much detail of what is after all, her business—"

Pip waved her hand.

"Gillan has a mutie self, lass," Edgar put in. "Her man, Branok, hasn't, but he comes of the Pendennis line—"

"Who *do*," Pip said. "Jamie is one and his dad and grandad have dog-selves."

"Eh, you're a sharp one. Gillan wed Branok hoping to—" He glanced at Joan.

"Reinforce the gene," Joan said. "It worked. Both their sons are muties. Now *our* den . . . our family line, so to speak, practises the same strategy. The Treadwells have a long history of a specific mutability. It *may* exist in other families, but so far we've never found it."

"So you chose Edgar—no, must have been the other way round, since *he's* the Treadwell."

"We both are, lass," Edgar said. "Kissing cousins, you might say." He blew a kiss to Joan.

"Treadwell bred and Treadwell wed," Joan added. "We aim for big families and in every generation a big percentage of us *wed out* to bring in fresh genes. We disclose first, of course. No nasty shocks then. Edgar and I are kissing cousins, at three removes. I have the mutability to a fair extent. Edgar has one of the most extreme I've ever met." She grinned at her husband.

"So what are you?" Pip was getting tired of the build-up.

"Guess," Joan said.

Pip sighed. She liked Joan and she *really* liked Edgar, but she had things to do in the city. Still . . . she was *trying* to be more flexible when it came to other people. She suddenly thought of the bucket they'd given her back in April, which they'd been discussing before this peculiar offshoot conversation began. *Really?* She thought of the person—manifestation—they suggested she might meet. *Trollie*. Really, then.

"I guess you're trolls," she said as steadily as she could.

"Reet, lass!" Edgar laughed again.

"You don't—no, of course you don't eat people or turn to stone in sunlight."

"Don't lurk under bridges to scare the goats, either," Joan

said.

"Sleep out under one, now and again," Edgar murmured.

Joan gave him a *look* that suggested sleeping wasn't all they did.

Really? Really.

"Show me, then," Pip said.

"You go first, love," Edgar said.

Joan put her hand out and Pip took it. Joan's handsome face broadened, and her clear olive skin greened to a grassy hue beyond that of even the leprechaun gossoons Pip had seen. Her eyes widened and glared, and shining flat scales layered themselves across her cheeks. Her hand, now a large, green-scaled paw, gave Pip's a companionable squeeze. "There now—" Her voice was gruff and gravelly. "Not too scary?"

Pip contemplated her. "No. Because I know it's you and you're still wearing your floaty top and pearls. *No one* can be scared of a troll maid wearing a floaty top and pearls."

Joan smiled, showing fine tusks. Slowly, the green faded, and she was handsome Joan again. "Grand. Now, love—" She nodded to Edgar.

Edgar pushed back his chair and turned to face Pip. "Not to worry, lass . . ." He turned away.

The change, unlike with Joan, was instant. Pip was pleased to note that although the already huge Edgar grew larger, at least his clothing was loose enough so he didn't pop buttons and rip seams. He was much less recognisable than troll-Joan. Pip looked up into his ferocious face. His eyes, black and frightening, fixed on her. His tusks, far larger than Joan's, bared in a savage grin. His skin, surely as tough as a dinosaur's hide, gleamed like polished chrysoprase.

"What do we have here . . . a tasty morsel for supper?" he growled.

"Now, now, Trollie," Joan chided. "We are not going to eat

Pippin. Pippin is our friend."

The beast turned on her. "Silence, *trollfrau*. I could swat thee—"

"I know you could, but you won't, without my say-so. And you know I'd swat you back." Joan laughed. "Cut the histrionics, Trollie. We have company."

"The morsel."

"This morsel is Pippin Pearmain," Pip said.

"It speaks. I like it."

The troll laughed uproariously. He reached out a hand the size of a breadboard and patted Pip's head gently. "Fay touched. Can't eat that."

"What?"

"He means you've been living with fay for a while," Joan interpreted.

"That'd be the cats."

"I like cats." The tusks curved like wicked scimitars.

"I doubt if they like you."

"They don't," Joan said, "but mark my words, if you have an angry and evil-minded fay cat to transport, Trollie's the troll for the job. His skin is claw-proof and his ears are howl-proof. He tries to soothe them with lullabies and he's never lost one yet." She nodded to the beast. "That's enough, Trollie. Let's have Edgar again."

"Kiss first."

"Oh, for—" Joan let go of Pip's hand and slowly assumed her troll form. She got up from the table and went to face her husband's other self.

Pip wondered if she ought to look away, but before she could do so, the giant dropped to his knees, took Joan's hands and kissed them gently. "Mein frau."

"My romantic old Trollie. Now, off you go. Edgar will want to talk to our guest."

The couple returned to hob-normal, with Edgar back to his

usual self before Joan.

They resumed their seats, and Joan lifted two teapots, one in each hand. "More tea?"

"Thank you." Pip indicated the one with the Indian tea. She usually avoided strong tea, but this time she thought she'd make an exception.

"Have you much planned in the city, love?" Joan asked, offering a plate of fat rascals.

"Quite a bit." Pip tried to sound unruffled. "I'm going to the Fairy Gardens first. Do you know them?"

"We know them well," Joan said.

"Good bridge there," Trollie growled, surfacing briefly.

Joan laughed. "Even so, whenever we go, there seems to be something new to see."

After that momentous morning tea, Edgar carried Pip's luggage up to her room.

"Do you want a lift anywhere, lass?" Joan asked.

"No thanks. I'll make my own way . . . there are taxies on Glebe Point Road?"

"Bound to be," Joan said.

"Grand."

"*Guten tag,*" Edgar murmured.

Pip took her leave of the couple and ventured off to follow the rest of her program.

Trolls now . . . who'd have thought it? And why the German — oh. Did they interbreed with alpenfee? I'd better read those books a lot more thoroughly when I get my own copies.

She'd borrowed the *Orders of the Fay* set from Edgar and Joan on her previous visit, but although she'd been allowed to take it with her to Delphinium Island, she hadn't found time to finish all the volumes before she had to fly home.

She put the matter out of her mind, more or less, except to remember she'd intended to ask the couple about the large fay cat she'd encountered on her first visit. Could that creature possibly be one of the cats Trollie transported?

Chapter Five. The Fairy Gardens Revisited

First off she made the visit to the Fairy Gardens in Windhill, the place she'd worked on when blocking *Delphine*. She'd also met the Dames with Dogs group there, which had led to her encounter with the St Ives family and thence to the offer of a fay puppy.

Pip had a lot to thank the gardens for, but today she intended to refresh her memory of the wooden statues of the gardens' founders. They'd been modelled by a sculptor named Xavier Partridge.

She got out of the taxi and dismissed the driver, because she wanted to take her time. The flag-fall for a new taxi was bound to be lower than the cost of keeping one hanging around.

She stood at the gate into the gardens, gazing up at the carving of the super-life-sized couple who were holding hands and stepping forth into their future.

Jacobi and Barbara le Fay were still alive. Pip hadn't met them, but Magda knew the family, being friends with Barbie's daughter Pandora.

The statues, Pandora had explained, were modelled from a photograph taken back in the 1950s.

Pip tilted her head back, focusing on their youthful faces. They looked happy and confident, with Barbara facing forward and Jacobi angling his head to look at her.

Pip sighed, partly with pleasure at the beautiful carving

and partly with a formless regret that she had never been part of a couple.

Parallel lives.

She reread the plaque telling a little of the le Fay story and re-checked the sculptor's name. Then she took out her first-generation Pink Princess phone and stated scrolling through her contacts.

"Xavier," she muttered. "Why would anyone want to be parked at the end of the alphabet?"

"I've sometimes wondered that myself," a pleasant voice remarked.

Pip almost dropped her phone.

She looked up and saw the speaker—a dark-haired man leaning against one of the statues.

"That's a bit disrespectful," she said.

"What, speaking to a stranger, or leaning on Jacobi? He wouldn't care." The man smiled and turned his head.

Pip spotted a slightly pointed ear.

Okay – he's fay. Pointed ears, so pixie, pisky or elf.

She discounted pisky because he wasn't wearing silver jewellery. His skin wasn't the olive typical of pixies, so she plumped for the most likely option.

"Master, are you an elf?"

His eyes widened.

"I won't mention it again if you're pretending to be human."

"I'm not. Not pretending. And we call it *passing.*"

Pip nodded. She remembered that.

He went on, "And yes, I'm an elf. Why did you ask?"

Pip said, smugly, "I have a set of encyclopaedias. I'm getting into practice at spotting your people."

The man lifted both hands in pantomimed dismay. "Flipping Piers does it again."

"I—"

"Piers le Fay, may his helmet pinch his estimable ears.

29

You're referencing his *Orders of the Fay* series, right? Probably the deluxe edition with the pictures by Pen Inkersoll. I won't wish anything nasty on *her* ears. Pen is simply doing her job. It's down to Piers that the thing exists at all."

Pip nodded with mentally raised eyebrows. She caught a faint and pleasant scent of marmalade as the elf man gestured. She couldn't tell if he was serious or not. Probably *not*, she thought. Elves could do exasperation, but the ones she knew didn't display resentment. Something went *click* in her mind.

"Never mind that now—might you be Master Xavier Partridge from Marmalade Woodcraft?"

"I'm not *from* it. I *am* it. Why—oh! Are you the excitable lady who wanted me to make her a bucket?"

"I am she. So, Frances passed on my message. I thought she might have forgotten. Why didn't you call me?"

"I've been trying to call you for a couple of days, ever since we got home."

"Oh." Pip remembered she'd been at the fossmere, where phones didn't work. She poked her phone and pulled up the seldom-used message bank to find a number of missed call notifications, as well as the still-unread message from Magda.

Giving up on that, she looked up hopefully at the elf man. "Okay. I'm Pippin Pearmain. I usually live in Jellico Bay, in Tasmania, but I've just come through the castle bridge gate. You know it?"

"It's my local."

"You use it often?"

"Yes. We—my wife and I—spend our weekends *over there*. We sort of live in two places. Nel has a job in the city. Well, mostly. We've just come back from a—"

"Trip on a galleon. *I* know. Frances said. So, will you make me a bucket, Master Partridge?"

"If that's what you want. I take all sorts of commissions, from tart-hutches to cradles to tea-trays to statues of distant relatives like Jacobi here." He patted the statue. "What kind of bucket? Functional or decorative? Do you have a sketch? What style? What wood? What—"

Pip held up her palm to stop the flow of questions. "I just want a beautiful bucket to add to my bucket list. Obviously, it needs to be functional, so no artistic holes."

"Um—buckets always have at least one hole. It's at the top. There are often hinge holes for the handles."

Pip gave him an old-fashioned look. "Now you're being silly."

He smiled. "A bit, maybe. Do forgive me. I just got off a galleon."

That was a non sequitur if ever Pip heard one, but she pushed on.

"No *extra* holes of the leaky variety. Apart from that, I'm open to suggestions."

"You're leaving it to me, then." He looked warily pleased.

"That's right. Entirely. I'm sure I can trust you to make what I want."

"Um. Thanks. Why?"

Pip beamed at him. "You're an elf. In *Delftvolk, Elves, Fijord-fee and Fisherfolk* it says elves are reckoned the most user-friendly of the major orders. Besides, I know three *and* one I think is a halfling, and they're all lovely."

"Hmm. I'd plead the fifth on that, if we actually had one. Piers is not necessarily lovely. Mind you *he's* a halfling. The other half is courtfolk, which probably explains it."

Pip was about to object to his order-profiling when she recalled she'd been doing that herself. The fay did it a lot, but they didn't seem to think it derogatory. Instead, she considered the three courtfolk she knew. Two of them were inclined to be courteous but pleased with themselves and gently amused by other people. The other was the kindest person she'd ever known. Still, she nodded.

Xavier probably had a point.

He went on, "But yes, I'll make you a beautiful bucket. Just one question—do you want elegant simplicity or lots of flowers and vines and things?"

"I want it pretty. Carved or painted, or—whatever will gladden my eyes."

"I can do pretty. My wife does pretty—um—look!"

He clicked his fingers and held out a carved figure of a woman in a Bo-Peep style dress painted in rose-pink and green. She had dark hair and was posed with her hands outstretched. "This is my wife the way she looked on our wedding day," he said. "She got the dress especially to gladden *my* eyes—I love pink."

"So do I. And I see you understand *pretty,* and how it has nothing to do with *sweet* or *cute* or *twee.* How do we do this? Will you post it to me? Or should I collect it? I'm getting a puppy in a few weeks, and I'll probably be back here in July, so I could maybe get the bucket then."

"I'll let you know when it's done, and we can decide what's best for delivery," he said.

"Brilliant. How much?"

"You have a budget?"

"Of course I have a budget. But I want this bucket. Most of my buckets are words and sketches. I'm making a proper book of them when I get more time. I had a lovely bucket for a few days, but I gave that to my cousin to put her sister in. Her ashes, I mean. It was the right thing to do. Now I have a nice trolls-in-fairyland bucket, but I want a *custom* bucket that can be mine forever. I may even want to inhabit it myself when I go to glory. In the manner of speaking."

His face lit up. "Oh, *that* sort of bucket. A once and future bucket of glorious inevitability. A bucket above and beyond the boundaries of buckethood. The bucket of a lifetime."

"*That* sort of bucket," Pip agreed.

He named a price. "Might be less. Won't be more. And I promise you, it will be the prettiest bucket you have ever seen."

Pip nodded. "Send me an account, or else I can pay when I get the bucket." She took out her feint-lined pad, unsnapped the pen and wrote down her address. "Here." She tore out the page. "And please thank Frances most sincerely for passing on the message. I was thinking all kinds of uncharitable things about her. In fact, I was considering calling her again when you turned up."

"I'll tell her." He took the address, stood back, and applied a critical gaze over the statues before nodding. "They're still okay. I like to check on them every so often. They were the biggest commission I'd had when I made them. They paid for our wedding." He kissed the carving of his bride and dismissed it. "I'll be in touch, Mistress Pearmain."

"Miss. I'm human."

He beamed at her. "So's my Nelis. And her mum, Daisy. And her dad, Snow — now, *he's* as weird as they come, but I like him. He has a yak-hair suit, made from ecologically-sourced combings in Tibet. He didn't wear it to our wedding."

CHAPTER SIX. CLOUDS OF HEAVEN

With her custom bucket practically in the bag, Pip caught a bus. She got off at Circular Quay and soon lost herself in a maze of narrow streets.

Seated in a café called *Der Kaffeetanz* and served with toast and cambric tea by a girl in a dirndl . . . but not one of the three she knew from the festival . . . Pip finally read Magda's message.

Good to catch up, Pippin. Hope you enjoy your time over there. Regarding the documentary, are you okay with the filming at your cottage on July third?

Pip, to her surprise, found that she was. The cottage had been her private refuge, but now Clarkia was there for the foreseeable future, and she had another refuge—a place where she could feel renewed and refreshed.

And maybe there would be another one, someday.

She wanted to see Alain again. She wanted to see his estate, and to stay in his manor, and to ride a mare called Lovely. Not for always, or even for a foreseeable future, but it would be nice to include Île de lin in her list of *favourite places to be*.

And I want to see his carved bucket and listen to him play his lute. And I'll take him a present . . . maybe some camomile tea or a Jellico diamond set in a silver pin. Or would that be inappropriate?

She thought it would have been all wrong as a gift for a human male friend, but the fay had different mores and assumptions. It wasn't as if she expected him to wear it. It would just be a souvenir.

Tea or Jellico diamond?

She was aware that this might prove academic. The van der Strands might be unwilling to take a message. It might be too difficult to get to Flaxen Isle. Alain's offer might have been made on a kindly impulse which he'd regret.

Pip went cold at the idea of belatedly accepting an invitation someone regretted making—especially Alain, who had always been her perfect memory friend.

"I wish I could know if he meant it," she said aloud.

"Meant what, mistress?" The dirndl girl was back beside her, holding a plate of cake with a towering crown of cream.

"I didn't order that," Pip said.

Dirndl Girl gestured towards four women sharing a table at the other side of the café.

For a moment Pip wondered if they were some of the Dames with Dogs who had recognised her, or maybe people she'd met at the festival, but a quick inspection told her she hadn't seen them before—at least, not as a group. One of them *did* look familiar—maybe someone she'd seen Dancing in the Dawn.

She looked them over with more attention. They weren't girls, but women in their twenties or thirties.

One was ethereal and fair in a hyacinth blue gown with extravagant lacy frills. Pip definitely approved. The outfit was a little light for winter, so Pip mentally added a fleecy shawl. The slender, dark-haired woman next to her wore jeans with a hoodie. Pip recognised that style of garment because Clarkia favoured it. The third was buxom and rosy-cheeked in a rather slinky dress patterned like oil on water, and the fourth had a dark blue vest over a yellow shirt. That one was fierce and hardly bigger than Pip herself. *She* was the one Pip had seen . . . surely with a tall blond man at the festival.

Ah! Pip mentally snapped her fingers. She'd been one of the presenters—a ballroom dancer in a swishy gold peacock dress. She hadn't quite recognised her in mufti.

As Pip examined them, the buxom one gave her a grin and a two-fingered wave.

Pip looked up at Dirndl Girl for an explanation.

"Penny, Amice, Anemone, and Angel wanted me to give you this," Dirndl Girl said, hefting the plate. Her name-tag announced her as Riva.

Pip looked doubtfully at the concoction. It smelled delicious, but it seemed odd that four strangers wanted to buy her a treat. "Why? Is it *be kind to little old ladies* week?"

Riva rolled her eyes. "I would like to say it's because they are charming ladies who want to spread the love. That's almost true, by the way. At least, one of them is charming. The other three are betrothed to three brothers. They are plotting to get the charming one over the line with a romantic gentleman who doesn't know his arse from his elbow. That was Penny's term, I'm afraid. She grew up with the gentleman concerned and she is somewhat forthright in her manner."

Pip had no quarrel with that. Forthright was good, unless the situation called for devious.

"I think they're planning on a quadruple wedding with three hundred roses and a hundred tulips. Penny insists on the tulips."

"My mum liked tulips. A friend and I planted some in her garden just last month. It was a bit late, but better later than not at all." She paused to contemplate just *how* late it had been. Then she asked, "But what has a quadruple wedding got to do with me and this cake?"

Riva's eyes rolled the other way. "They made a bet with the universe. So to speak. Angel—that's the little one, and you do *not* cross her if you want to live—she said you were a lady who had the stamina to eat a large slice of *Wolken des Himmels*. Penny said you hadn't, and you couldn't, and even if you could, you wouldn't. Amice twittered in a ladylike fashion, and Anemone—that's the dark one, and the one I'd regard as most sensible, though I don't know her well — said to ask you. So, in the interests of full disclosure, this is a large slice of Clouds of Heaven cake made to an old family recipe. It has seven fruits for the seven hues of heaven, seven spices, and pure unsweetened cream that has not been combined with anything but air. It is not for the fainthearted or for the finicky stomached. It contains gluten, eggs, lactose, fructose, butterfat, and probably traces of seeds and nuts."

"And what happens if I eat it?" Pip asked. The cake smelled as good as it looked, and she'd been very well exercised at the fossmere. The plain toast she'd ordered with her tea had barely touched the sides.

Riva rolled her eyes merrily. "Liebling, if you eat it, Angel has promised to visit Thorold Fitzmaurice — that really *is* his name — and deliver unto him a proposal of marriage. I think she will also explain to him the proverb of birds in the hand. She will do it well, and she will be believed. I guarantee Fitz will want to write an answer just to remove Angel from his doorstep. And it will be good for him to be on the receiving end for a change."

"Angel wants to be with this Fitz?"

"No, Angel has a man already. If he is anything like his brother, who is betrothed to Penny, he might possibly eat Fitz for breakfast as the saying goes. It is Amice, the lady in blue, who will write the proposal. She is exactly what Fitz wants and what he needs. He's just too bockle-headed to see it. No. That's wrong. He does see it, I'm sure. He's just too bockle-headed to admit it."

Pip had another look at the woman in blue, who seemed to be in a maidenly flutter, or maybe just holding back hysterics. She raised her brows in query.

The maidenly one looked suddenly sensible and gave a tiny nod.

Go ahead.

Pip nodded back and reached for the cake.

The women at the table stared at Pip and the big one with the rosy cheeks laughed.

Pip gave them a *look*. "Ja. *Und?*" She plunged the fork into the *Wolken des Himmels*.

The four women applauded.

The cake was — out of this world. Pip ate it all, scraped the plate, rose and swept a *grand reverence* to the ladies. "I'll take another of those — to go."

Then she turned to Riva, who was watching with smiling admiration. "How many of you are fairies and what are your orders?"

Riva pointed to herself. "I'm Riva Bless. Alpenfee. Penny is kanaalfee, which is why she wants tulips. Amice is court-folk — a lady, but one of the sweet-natured ones. She usually looks pensive, but today she's a mix of hope and horror, I suspect. Angel and Anemone are human, as far as I know, but definitely fay-touched."

Pip, who was fay-touched herself, on account of living with the cats, nodded her approval.

"And the unfortunate Master Fitzmaurice?"

"Courtfolk. And he's not unfortunate, except that he's all alone and rattling around in a handsome manor that ought to be filled with children. He and Amice are old acquaintances. She will be good to him, and he will be happy. Amice is an excellent cook, a conscientious gardener, her stillroom is second to none, and she thinks him every bit as fine as he thinks himself. She has a loving and forgiving heart."

Pip relaxed. Old acquaintances. Very nice indeed. "Has he got a lute?"

The one called Amice leaned forward. "He has, mistress. She's called Dominia. He plays her beautifully, and he sings like a bird."

"He yowls," the one called Penny opined.

Pip had forgotten how sharp the fay hearing was. She

hoped she hadn't said anything offensive.

"Miss. Not mistress. I'm human. And I know two courtfolk men with lutes," she said.

The big one—Penny—laughed. "My dear, it's a condition of the creatures. Three out of four of them have lutes and most of them name the things. Dominia. I ask you!"

Pip resolved to find out what Alain's lute was called. She knew Court Leopold called his Lady Lyonesse, because Tamzin had told her. She also knew it was decorated with teapots. She rather approved of that.

Interesting though the conversation was, she had other fish to fry, so she finished her tea, wished the four conspirators luck, ordered a large cake *to go* to be collected on her way back to the bus, and headed out into the bright chill of a Sydney winter day.

What those women were doing was reprehensible, of course. But—two of them were fairies, and if the man with the lute didn't like the idea of accepting the sweet-faced blonde in the blue frock as his bride, he could always tell her *thank you but no.*

And Alain can always tell me *no . . . but he won't. He wouldn't have invited me if he didn't want me to come.*

CHAPTER SEVEN. LADY LANE

Pip wandered on, soaking up the delights of the harbour city before turning into a narrow byway called Lady Lane.

She was pondering some of the odd little shops and wondering if a Hebridean wool coat would be a good investment when a familiar voice hailed her.

She turned sharply and felt a smile break over her face as she recognised Tamzin Campania. Tamzin had her daughter on her hip and two dogs on a split leash, her fiddle on her back, and a wooden art case and a stuffed bear in her free hand, but far from looking overburdened she might have been strolling through the orchard on Delphinium Island weighed down by nothing but a smile.

"Pip! How lovely to see you!"

Pip held out her hands. "What may I take for you?"

Tamzin said, "If you *could* take the emperor and Shoe . . . and, if you can bear it, Fou's bear . . ."

Pip accepted the leash and the shabby but blessedly sweet-smelling stuffed toy and looked down at the dogs. She knew them slightly from the festival, and they seemed to recognise her. Fou the Pekingese looked up at her with enigmatic boot-button eyes, and Shoe, the terrier mix, who was Fou's daughter, bounced and braced her paws on Pip's knees, making and keeping eye-contact.

"Good morning, Your Imperial Majesty Fou. Greetings, Princess Shoe." Pip rubbed their heads and stuffed the bear in her messenger bag. She did it with care. Her dealings with Lupin's Cat had taught her that not every seemingly-

inanimate representation of an animal was exactly as presented. "Where are you heading?"

"To *Fairings* — you know — the shop that did the clothes for
the festival. I'm taking the dogs and Music to visit with Nanny
Lu while I go and talk business with a gallery. We're setting
up a display of my festival art."

Pip nodded, pleased. She'd got festival clothes from Asher
and Jessie in the vast transparent building called the Icehouse,
and she'd gathered Nanny Lu was Asher's mother who loved
little children and animals.

Tamzin, moving faster without the dogs, led the way. "I
also have an ulterior motive. I want to see what they can do
in the way of costumes for *Tales in Tune*. Are you coming to
launch the book?"

"We hope so. It seems we *might* go to print in time," Pip
said.

"Lovely! Remind me to give you the test-brochures we got
done . . . I just picked the samples up from the printer today,"
Tamzin said. "You can't guess how thrilled I am to be *this close*
to regaining a piece of my childhood. Those sample pics you
showed me on your phone brought so much back. Do you
know anything of the book's history and the fay connection?"

"The — " Pip cut herself off. She didn't approve of repeating
what someone else had just said. She added, "I suppose there
must *be* one. The pictures definitely show scenes from *over
there* — right?"

"The castle one and the waterfall one, certainly," Tamzin
said. "I'm not sure of the one of the cats — the one I was trying
to reproduce — but in the photo they look like schemers to
me."

Pip almost said, "Schemers?" but caught herself in time.
Instead, she said, "I don't understand that term in that context."

Tamzin said, "A few years ago, I was *over there* in a place called Île d'eté . . . or Summer Island. I stayed at the stable house that belongs to my friend Andy. He had cats—some visiting and some that lived there. He and Bluebell—another friend—used to call them *schemers*. They were phasers . . . fay cats. Not quite Schrödinger's cats, because they were undoubtedly alive, but . . . let's put it this way. You could *not* confine them. I believe if you put one in a safe and welded it shut—not that I ever would!—as soon as you cut a piece of cheese that cat would be out of the safe and winding around your ankles. Ah—here we are." She indicated an arched doorway hung with a rainbow of scarves.

Pip hesitated, but the dog Fou, who had been moving sedately at the prescribed Pekingese pace, suddenly clapped on sail and towed her on into the shop and through a hanging curtain.

Nanny Lu, who looked like a wary human but who must be at least partly an elf, had been embroidering, but she put aside her work, bent, and stretched out her arms in greeting. "Darling Fou and Shoe!"

The dogs went to snuggle against her and Pip, feeling superfluous, handed over their leash and the bear.

Nanny Lu greeted her with an abstracted smile, but her attention was mostly on the dogs.

Pip retreated into the main part of the shop and gazed around, entranced by gleaming fabrics, soft music that sounded like lullabies and the sweet scents of flowers and baking. It was all so *pretty*. The clothing at the festival had been lovely, but the Icehouse had been noisy and full of activity. This shop was a haven of serene possibility.

She turned to Tamzin, who was setting her daughter on her feet.

"Nanny Lu?" the little girl said.

"Just through there, sweeting." Tamzin indicated the curtain, and Music ran off.

Tamzin said to Pip, "Nanny Lu *loves* children. And dogs. It's her vocation as much as her embroidery. In another life she might have been a kindergarten teacher." She turned to the young man behind the counter. "Hi, Asher. You're holding the fort today? Where are Jacaranda and Jessie?"

"They've gone to the market. Greet you, Miss Pip. Lovely to see you again. Are you looking for something special?"

Pip intended to say she wasn't looking for anything, but she remembered the unerring eye for colour and form Asher had shown at the festival. If word ever got out concerning this young man and his talent for matching clothes and wearers, he could end up being a stylist to the stars. Pip had never regarded herself as a star . . . more of a jobbing niche-market performer, but she *had* starred in *Queen of the Clowder*. She was still wearing her riding clothes, and possibly smelled of horse, but Fimber was a healthy creature, and she doubted if Asher was sensitive to clean, natural scents.

Tamzin said, "I don't know what Pip needs, but *I* need something for *Tales in Tune*." She glanced at Pip. "I really hope there's a story character in your book to give me inspiration. I wish I could remember more. Whatever it is, it needs to be wearable, and preferably something that doesn't look like a dress you'd buy in the high street."

Pip said, "There's a story called *Flowers for the Forest*. It tells of a fairy woman who goes into a dark forest where all the flowers are asleep. She plays her music, and the sun shines through the canopy. The flowers wake. I always loved that one because there was an apple tree that came into blossom. Because it was a tree, it was a sort of bridge between the forest and the flowers. Do you remember that one?"

Tamzin shook her head regretfully.

"The fairy wears a dress in shades of green with a cape made out of flowers, and I think she has a gold circlet with leaves on it. It's difficult to tell, because her hair is woven through it."

"Jacaranda could do the dress and cape," Asher said.

Tamzin said, "And *I* know a goldsmith who will make me a circlet. Thank you, Pip. That's perfect."

Chapter Eight. Brochures and Book Babies

Some hours later, stuffed with information, impressions and carrying a *Fairings* bag and a high-rise cakebox containing her Clouds of Heaven, Pip returned to the guesthouse.

Edgar and Joan welcomed her kindly. Trolls were not mentioned. However, Pip found an opportunity to ask them the question that had been teasing her mind for a while and which she'd forgotten to ask after her encounter with the Treadwells' other selves.

"When I stayed here before—with Magda—you took me through the gate for my ballet practice," she said to Edgar.

"Aye."

"And you got me back through again. Felicity Dark brought me through this morning. Magda said you needed a fair helping of fay blood to open the gate, but I remember someone saying people—humans—sometimes get *over there* by mistake."

Joan nodded sagely. "It happens occasionally. Usually the people concerned are rather strong trace fay."

"I heard about one human who got washed through the Bass Strait gate . . ." Pip realised she'd better not discuss Zach and Jisinia's business, so she hurried on. "Just before Magda and I left for Delphinium Island, I went round in the courtyard and opened the gate. Just in case I *could*."

"Eh, I'm guessing you wound up in t'neighbour's yard," Edgar said.

"Sort of. The neighbour wasn't there, but I met a gardener and a tomcat. The gardener said the cat didn't live with him, but he was *obviously* a fay tom."

"That would be Rasputin, I expect, and the man might have been Raphael Angelus," Joan said.

"It was Rasputin, but the man was called Gabriel. Never mind him, though. I wanted to ask you how many fay cats there are *over here*. I live with two of them, as I told you, but they can't, or won't tell me how they got to Lemonwood Cottage except that it wasn't through the Bass Strait gate. I'd know that anyway. They're not too fond of water . . . other than to drink. Having them not explain things isn't unusual. They don't tell me about anything they don't want me to know."

"Tell you?" Joan asked.

"Yes." Pip explained about Cat-Morse. "I can't tell you how it works, and I thought for a while I was imagining it . . . and the cats, maybe . . ."

"But not now," Joan said.

"No. My acceptability or suspension of disbelief or whatever is rapidly expanding. But how many *are* there?"

Edgar said, "Not so many as you might think, lass. Most of them stay with fay living this side o' the gate, but some attach themselves to your folk. As for Rasputin, we think he must ha' slipped through the courtyard gate as a kitten."

"What—following someone?"

"Could be," Joan agreed. "Or just wandered through on his own. Some cats don't seem to need gates." She shrugged.

"No accounting for t' beasties," Edgar commented. "Joan's mam had cats, some fay, some not, but all unaccountable."

"You don't have any."

Edgar's friendly face blinked out of view as he metamorphosed into his second self. "I like cats," Trollie growled. His fearsome gaze fixed on Pip. "Guten tag, morsel. Still not

46

eating thee."

Joan, seeming unruffled, said, quietly, "Trollie, it's Edgar's turn."

"Always is," the troll groused.

"Not always. We might go trysting under the bridge some-day soon . . . *if* you can be patient." She reached out for his huge paw and raised it to her lips.

The troll's face split into a delighted grin — and Edgar was back.

"Sorry, lass," he rumbled, apparently addressing Joan and giving her hand a squeeze before restoring it to her. "Was the mention o' your mam's cats that did it."

After that small episode, Pip decided *not* to ask if Trollie had ever encountered Rasputin and if so, who had won. She was betting that if it had ever happened, the battle would have been royal, but some things were designed to stay a mystery.

After supper, she spent the night in the familiar room that smelled of parkin and pears, back with the flowery curtains and chair which reminded her of Little Mum and her love of all things floral.

Next morning, despite a desire to beg Edgar to take her through the gate to dance with Jane one more time, she did her practice in her room, restricting herself to exercises, then farewelled the Treadwells and caught an early train. She had the gut feeling that if she *had* returned to the fossmere, she'd have wanted to stay on for one more day, then for another . . . and she did have her real life to consider.

She flew home, where Jan fetched her from the airport.

The cats made no comment about a lack of cheese while she'd been gone, and indeed Kittisack looked suspiciously plump, but Pip didn't like to mention it.

Over an afternoon tea featuring the impressive cake, which Pip was almost too tired to eat, Jan promised to send Pip a beta copy of her new manuscript to read.

Her second book, *Garterstakes,* had arrived from *The Orange Grove* along with three sets of the *Orders of the Fay* while Pip was away.

Pip unpacked the box of books and promptly gave one set to Jan, who seemed pleased but a wee bit bemused to be handed what must have seemed a random present of an encyclopaedia of creative mythology.

"Ja? *Und?*" Pip asked with hauteur.

"It's *lovely,*" Jan said hurriedly, tracing the green and gold figuring on the boxed set. "This reminds me actually . . . the Hot Unicorns say the advance copies of *Grandmother's Sunshine will* be printed by the end of this month."

"That's —"

"That's most odd, I agree," Jan said. "But it didn't need to go through multiple edits — or any edits at all. It just needed a proofing to check the OCR was okay. Apparently they decided to print locally for expediency. Two of them are doing the parental leave thing with their partners when the bumps arrive. They wanted to be ready. They furthermore asked if the offer of an external launch next month still stands."

"It stands," Pip said. She explained that she'd met Tamzin and Music in the city before catching the train. She didn't think it necessary to inform them that she'd acquired a new dress in a soft shade of what she thought of as sunrise-pinkish-gold. Its skirt fell like a bell tutu, making it perfect for dancing, and it had sleeves to the elbow and a gently scooped neck bound with braid and decorated with daisies.

It wasn't precisely a costume from the book, but it vaguely resembled a character from a little song called *Spinner of Dreams.* All she'd need was a spindle

Pip felt fabulous in it, although she had no idea when or even if it would be seen in public.

She tugged her mind away from gratuitous and glorious

frocks and back to the renaissance of books.

"Grand," Jan said. "I'll tell the Unicorns."

"It would be easier if they deal directly with *Arts in Tune*," Pip said. She pulled out her feint-lined pad and tore off a page which bore the contact information Tamzin had given her. "If they call or email Matin Campania, he'll discuss all the logistics with them. It'll be much less complicated than trying to run as a go-between."

I'll wear it to the festival as my costume. Maybe, even on my Amateur Acclaim *appearance. Amateur celebrates doing things for the love of it and that includes lovely things.*

Oops. Her mind had skittered back to her sunrise dress.

Jan looked doubtful on the matter of delegation, but working with Sully for all those years had taught Pip it was often better to find someone trustworthy then to leave matters in their hands. Pip trusted Tamzin. Tamzin trusted Matin. Jan trusted the Hot Unicorns.

"If you're sure," Jan said.

"Definitely." Pip again banished visions of her new dress.

Vanity, thy name is Pippin . . . and watch out for your fingers and toes. If you carry on like this, the universe might even give you a bruised nose and two black eyes.

She pulled the brochures out of her messenger bag. "These are the advance brochures Tamzin gave me for *Tales in Tune* with a mock-up for the launch, supposing it goes ahead. One for each of you — along with the declaration you need to sign — and one for the Hot Unicorns. Are they going to be at the launch?"

"Probably just Dirk, I should think. He doesn't have a partner preparing to launch the new generation, so he has more time to think of book babies. And yes, two of the Unicorns actually do call them that."

"Give this to Dirk, then, and make sure he okays or counter-proposes for the ad and signs up for the festival newsletter," Pip said. "Tell him he is welcome to bring a costume to fit the theme, or he can just report to the Icehouse, and some-one will fix him up with a festival shirt that will also advertise the Hot Unicorns. You and Clarkia — the same applies."

Jan gave her an awed look. "Glory, Pippin — what's got into you?"

Pip stared at her, nonplussed.

"You've got *organised*," Jan said.

"Ja. *Und*? I've always been organised."

Jan blinked. "You have, but all that slithering sideways from committing yourself made it seem you weren't."

Only a close relative could have made that summation, Pip thought. Since it was true, she could hardly blame Jan for voicing it.

"By the way." Jan clearly wanted to change the subject, so Pip let her. "Clarkia has been showing me some of the stuff you two have been sorting, including a crate that seems to hold a bushel or so of plush cats. Obviously, I saw only the top layer since it hasn't been unpacked. Would you like to have the other plush cats back? The ones you gave me for Clarkia and which I forgot to give to her?"

"*Neglected* to give to me, Mum," Clarkia growled.

"You would have dribbled on them."

Pip recalled Tane saying much the same thing regarding the putative copy of *Grandmother's Sunshine* she intended to give to his baby son. But she'd still give it to him. Tiny Tallien deserved beautiful books, even though he already lived in the most beautiful place she knew.

She said, bracingly, "Toys and books *should* be given to children. There is no point in putting them away until *later*, because *later* might never come. Think of our *Grandmother's Sunshine* books. I can't remember when Little Mum gave mine to me, so I must have been very young. I also can't remember her saying I mustn't read it with jammy hands or take it into the garden. Mum and Aunt Helen had them before us, and

Little Nanna Laurel before them, and probably her mother before her, right back to Cammie and Callie.

"That's a *lot* of potentially sticky little paws turning those old pages, and yet they're in good condition."

"I did intend to give the cats to Clarkia," Jan protested. "Anyway, do you want them back?"

"No. There's no point storing them forever."

"You never know," Jan said optimistically, "one day there might be a Pippin Pearmain Museum, dedicated to the dancing centenarian."

"So there might," Pip said. "Anyway, get that Unicorn saddled up and see if he can deliver as promised. We don't want a book launch with no books."

Jan looked down at the brochure. "Hey, this line-up of workshops looks good. I bet a lot of authors I know would like to attend. Using music to enhance stories is an idea as old as time, but I've never heard of a festival that focused on it."

"Your writing friends had better get tickets, then," Pip said, remembering what Matin had said when he spoke of available spots . . . or had he just meant for vendors? "There's accommodation onsite, and meals."

She wondered if Piers le Fay, the author of *Orders of the Fay* would attend, and maybe Tamzin's friend Emily Scarborough, whose fantasy series Tamzin was illustrating. Maybe even Humph's son, anonymous author of a 1990s series . . . That put her in mind of something else.

"Will you and the Unicorns want to launch *Garterstakes* as well?"

"I don't see how we can," Jan said. "Our association with *Grandmother's Sunshine* will be transparent, but Jan Sharman is *not* what readers expect to see if they meet Juniper Jin."

"It can be done as a separate entity," Pip said. "Do you remember me mentioning Humph? He's the playwright who wrote *Half-Life of the Lost*. It turns out he also wrote the script of *House of Heriot,* under a penname. One of his sons is the author of a really high-profile series from the nineties, but it's not generally known. So, you *could* have a launch for *Garter-stakes,* and still stay incognito. It takes place at a wedding, right? You could incorporate wedding music."

"Maybe," Jan said. "I'll run it by them. But how do *you* know of this other author, since it's a secret?"

"Star Calder-Quince told me. She and Humph are both members of Biblio-Rep, and he has trouble with facial recognition, so it's possible he let it slip to her thinking she was someone who knew already. He invited a vintage film star to be in *Half-Life,* thinking he was a contemporary musician, so anything is possible."

"Hm." Jan seemed to accept that, and it did seem likely to Pip. Humph might have mentioned his son's books to *anyone* by mistake. It was lucky he'd chosen Star, who had enough integrity to keep quiet. Mostly.

Jan examined the brochure and a small frown appeared between her eyes. "The title's not mentioned here. It just says *Book Launch.*"

"Yes. I asked Tamzin what was going on there. She said it covers other books that might be launched in the same window. Keeping the titles a mystery means more people will show up from curiosity, and also allows for impromptu entries. There's a little book called *Orders of Field and Forest,* by the same author as the *Orders* series I gave you, and possibly some others."

"Seems sensible," Jan allowed. "I'll have to see what the Hot Unicorns say regarding *Garterstakes.*"

She put down the brochure and changed the subject. "By the way, I brought that jewellery of Nanna Laurel's to show you."

CHAPTER NINE. BROOCHES

Jan opened her lavender print bag and took out a shabby leather zip-up case.

Pip realised she recognised it from days spent at Little Nanna Laurel's place. She watched with mild interest as Jan undid the zip and opened out the case. It was lined with faded green velvet, and the items it contained were clipped to it with small safety pins.

There were two necklaces of carnival glass, a gold watch, three pairs of clip-on floral earrings, and two brooches — one a ceramic flower that might have been intended as a schizanthus bloom, and one gold bar brooch with a safety chain.

"This is it," Jan said. "Mum never had it appraised, and I doubt if Lupin bothered either. She wore the bar brooch, as you probably remember. I know a wee bit about vintage costume jewellery because the main characters in *Garterstakes* went shopping for an engagement ring at estate sales. I'm no expert, but I think the gold brooch might be Georgian. The necklaces are vintage, possibly from the nineteen thirties. The flower brooch is probably late Victorian. The watch is from the sixties and the earrings . . . goodness knows, but twentieth century sometime. Enamel and Lucite. Pretty. I'd never wear them, but they'd look good on one of those collection boards."

"Thanks for showing me," Pip said. She agreed privately with Jan's theories. The gold brooch was probably the only piece with more than sentimental value — and indeed, it was the one piece she could remember Lupin wearing, although she thought Little Nanna had sometimes worn the watch and maybe the floral brooch.

Jan indicated the brooch and fished down her neck for a pendant Pip hadn't noticed before. "Magnifying glass," Jan said, sighing. "You don't know how lucky you are to have twenty-twenty vision."

Pip said, "I'm not sure I have. Haven't had an eye test since I got my drivers' licence."

"You must have good vision. You read without glasses. You might need this magnifier to see the name on the brooch, though."

She took off the chain with the lens suspended and handed it to Pip.

Pip raised the magnifier, leaned over and used it to examine the gold brooch. "C-A-L-A-N-T-H-E," she spelled out. "And what's this? A clover leaf with some sort of gemstone?"

"The stone is carnelian, and it's a flower, probably," Jan said, but it didn't look like a calanthe flower to Pip.

She said, "So we could have known Callie's name all along."

"I suppose so. First name, anyway. Lupin never said anything."

Pip handed the magnifying glass pendant back to Jan, who replaced it around her neck.

"Would you like anything?" Jan asked, indicating the collection.

"No thanks. I'm pleased to have seen them, but Lupin was your sister, and Aunt Helen was your mum, so they should definitely stay with you. Besides —" She didn't finish that sentence but glanced at Clarkia.

"Okay," Jan said. "But still, if I, or Clarkia, ever decide to sell them . . ."

"You can tell me, or not. They're *yours*."

Jan zipped up the case. "Noted. And now I'd better get home to Mark before he forgets what I look like."

So he is still in the picture.

Pip had been wondering for a while. Jan and Clarkia had mentioned him from time to time, but since Pip barely knew him, he hadn't featured greatly in conversations.

Jan went on, "Welcome home, Pip. I'll be in touch as soon as I've cornered that Unicorn." She gathered up her brochures and crammed them into her lavender print bag. "Bye, Pip. Bye, Clarkia, love . . . come and see us soon." She bent to stroke the cats who had gone to roost on the back of Pip's sofa. "Bye, Autumn and Unseelie. See you later, and don't mention the extra cheese to Pippin . . ." She bustled off, with Clarkia in tow.

Pip turned to the cats. "Cheese? *What* extra cheese?"

They gave her satisfied blinks.

Tell no one, Kittisack signalled.

He slid down from the sofa and left the room at the run.

Amberjill remained in her place. *The little dog has been born,* she remarked, purring. *He would want us to celebrate with cheese.*

Pip felt a ridiculously wide smile blooming over her face.

Chapter Ten. Time Behind

Tektite was a reality.

A few seconds after Amberjill's revelation, Pip's phone pinged with a message from Gillan St Ives, giving her confirmation of at least some of what the cats had said . . . she didn't mention celebrating with cheese.

The Shadowhond bitch named Maanlicht had produced a litter of four pups—three males and one female. They were fat little squeakers, Gillan wrote, all suckling well. The black cherry bitch pup was bespoken, but Pip could consider the three dog pups—an ash, a charcoal and an obsidian.

Photos might be a possibility if she borrowed an old-fashioned manual camera from a pixie man at KerryKenny, but the result would be uncertain, and they wouldn't be digital. Gillan said she would send a detailed description when the pups looked more like miniature dogs.

Pip rocked on her toes and used her marigold cup to toast her pup with Caraway's Cordial. Star had arranged for a catalogue as soon as she returned from the Escapade, and Pip made good and frequent use of it.

"You're looking pleased, Pip," Clarkia said, coming back inside after seeing Jan on her way. She sat down at the computer where she was creating a spreadsheet of what she termed The Potted Lives Collection.

"My puppy's been born."

And a goodly beast he will be, Lupin's cat remarked.

Clarkia looked interested. "What fun. Are you going to see him? Before he comes to live here, I mean?"

"I'd have to fly to the mainland."

"We're going to Sydney in less than four weeks anyway," Clarkia pointed out. "Actually, Pip, that would be the perfect time to see him if he's anywhere near Sydney. He'd be toddling around and looking like a puppy rather than a blob. Not much use if he's in the Northern Territory or Western Australia, of course. It'd cost an arm and a leg to get there."

"I could get to where he is from Sydney, so I'll do that," Pip decided. "If we all fly out together, you and Jan could go on to Delphinium Island and I can go out to where the pup is and follow you later."

"Do you know where to go?"

"No, but Gillan—the woman who arranged this for me—will give me directions, or even take me there."

"Where is it, exactly?"

"I don't know," Pip said honestly. "But Gillan lives in Sydney, and she has been to visit the litter, so it can't be too long a trip. She's already doing me a favour by making arrangements, but I doubt if she'd want to travel too far out of her way for a stranger."

"You could offer her petrol money and buy her lunch while you're there."

Pip didn't feel like explaining why that would be implausible.

"Sounds like a plan, anyway," Clarkia said. "Have you been in touch with your friend's nephew yet to ask him to cat-sit?"

Pip hadn't, but she said vaguely that it was on her to-do list.

She had no idea how to locate Jamie. *Jamie Pendennis* wasn't a John Smith name, but as a *very* young man he wouldn't be in the phone book.

She brightened. Star had said Candlemas was in touch with the girls from *Forever*, which meant she could contact Laura.

Laura would know how to find her brother.

Grand.

Easy-peasy.

Yet—where was the fun in that?

When Clarkia had gone to work, Pip produced the most evil smile of her repertoire and hit a number she had saved in her phone.

"V-S Office. Trip speaking."

Excellent.

"This is Pippin Pearmain."

There was a short pause before Geraint Trip said, "I hope you're not planning to hum at me, Miss Pearmain."

Pip realised with mild surprise that she rarely did that any more.

"I won't if you don't annoy me," she said. She wondered how the acerbic Lupin had really got along with Trip during their time as colleagues. Well enough, supposedly, since Trip and his wife Mary recalled her with affection.

"What may I do for you, then?" Trip asked.

"I want to borrow Jamie and Kakao."

"For what purpose?" He sounded cautious.

"What harm could a woman of my age do to a lovely lad and his dog? I want them to feed and entertain the cats while I go *over there* to visit a puppy, then down to *Tales in Tune* for a book launch or possibly two. After that, I may visit an old friend who lives at a place called Île de lin. That would depend on whether I have time, whether I have courage, and whether a seafay man with an alarming wife will help me out with messages. However, it all totally depends on whether I may borrow Jamie and Kakao. You see, my cousin, Clarkia is going to the book launch. She's the one who cat-sat while I was filming *Half-Life of the Lost* during *Dance in Tune*."

"I understand," Geraint Trip said.

"I thought you might. Amaryllis is your daughter, and Laura is your step-granddaughter, right?"

"And they danced in your *Queen of the Clowder* ballet, so I am aware of at least some of your activities. You *have* been busy, Miss Pearmain. Has anyone ever compared you with a wasp in a bottle? No? So am I to understand your Experience proved beneficial?"

"It was enormously beneficial. If you were here I would probably hug you in gratitude for forcing my hand. And I'm a person who doesn't normally hug."

The silence that followed was quite startled.

"I have a wife," Trip said primly.

"Ja. *Und*? Have you never heard of a hug of friendship? I'd probably hug your wife as well. I'm sure she's a darling. Amaryllis is, and she must have got it from *somewhere*."

The startled pause resumed.

Pip added, "I have a great deal to do as a consequence of the Experience. So may I please borrow Jamie and Kakao to mind the cats?"

"I have no idea."

"But I just explained why I need them."

"I understand that perfectly. What I don't understand is why you think *I* have any say in the matter."

"Didn't I explain?"

"I don't believe you did."

"Easy-peasy. I don't have his address." A sense of ill-usage returned. "When I wanted to talk to him to discuss the cats, Zach made the call instead of telling me the number."

"I'm glad someone was keeping to the rules," Trip said. "Otherwise, they seem to have been smithereened in all directions. Since you have a prior acquaintance with my grandson-by-love, I shall get in touch with him and have him call you *if* he chooses. Will that suffice?"

"I suppose so," Pip grudged. "Master Trip—"

"Miss Pearmain?"

"Never mind. But please ask him. He *said* he'd come to look after the cats if I needed him."

"In that case he probably will. Jamie and his sister are most reliable people. They get it from their mother."

Trip hung up.

Pip put her phone on the charger and sat down to wait for Jamie's call.

After a while she decided that was foolish. *A watched phone never rings.* She went into the garden to visit Bill blue-tongue and to check on the sentient lemon. Before she'd made it five steps along the path, the phone rang, and Pip scooted back in.

"Yes?" She juggled the phone, nearly dropping it in her haste.

"Miss Pearmain? Gerry said you wanted to talk to me."

"Jamie! Yes, thanks. Remember you said you'd come and look after the cats and the cottage again if I needed you?"

"Yes."

"I need you."

"When?"

Good answer.

Pip puffed out her cheeks. "Sometime in July."

"Okay. Let me know a few days beforehand. I'm based not far from you, so I can stay for as much time as you need and go to work from there."

"You won't . . . of course you won't."

"I won't leave the cottage and cats for more than a couple of hours, and I'll have Kakao tell them where I'll be."

"Kakao can communicate with them?"

"Sort of. I can't explain."

"Just the way you couldn't explain where Kakao was when I asked you before I — never mind. Am I allowed to have your number now?"

"I expect so. Gerry didn't say not, and he would have. Anyway, it will have shown up in this call log." Jamie gave it to her anyway.

"Thank you. The lemon tree will be glad to hear you're

coming."

Pip dusted off her hands and returned to the crates. She and Clarkia had by now unpacked, sorted, and listed nearly all of them. Little Mum's catalogues had been the tip of the family iceberg, paving the way for other things, once familiar.

Pip had a blurry memory of packing some of Little Mum's favourite things, along with Little Dad's odds and ends Little Mum had kept around for comfort before her flit. Three neat boxes, packed by Little Mum, held memorabilia from Pip's grandparents. A lot of it was from the Pearmain side of the family, because Aunt Helen had helped pack up when they lost Nanna and Pop Laurel. She must have kept some of their things, as she had every right to do.

In the *Laurel* box, Pip was enchanted to find a miniature metal bucket painted with a white flower, and the words Guelder Rose painted underneath. She wondered if it might have been Little Mum's, whose name had been Rose Guelder, but she couldn't remember seeing it before.

Little Nanna's *Herbal Lore* was there, inscribed to Schizanthus on her eighth birthday, from Grandmama Godsell.

Godsell, Pip thought, frowning. She went to find some family tree notes Clarkia had copied out for her. The surname *Godsell* appeared as Calanthe Darby's married name, and also regarding her son Har, whom Jan had thought was more likely a Harold or a Harley. If Har had a wife, then she would have been Little Nanna's grandmother. That made the book of herbs quite respectably old.

She examined it closely, but, as with *Grandmother's Sunshine,* there was no publication date.

She telephoned Jonquil Orange at *The Orange Grove* and asked if she had any copies of *Herbal Lore.*

"I have three books with that title," Jonquil said. "Which one did you want?"

Pip decided to come clean, as she had still not done

regarding *Grandmother's Sunshine.* "I don't *want* one. I *have* one. It belonged to my grandmother. I was wondering if it was well-known, that's all."

"If you describe it, I might be able to place it," Jonquil said patiently.

Pip inspected the book. "It doesn't have a dust-jacket. It has cream boards that have gone a kind of light timber colour, and a . . . embossed, or maybe debossed . . . illustration on the front. Looks like some kind of herb in the Umbelliferae family. Fennel, maybe."

"Author name?" Jonquil asked, still patiently.

"Hard to say. It looks as if it used to be gold-embossed or debossed, but it's very worn."

"Try inside the book."

"I did. It's not there. What *is* on the cover looks like *Cee Cee Ah.*"

"Aha, the mystery initials. That's a sort of half-way step between an actual pseudonym of the Currer Bell variety and the *By a Lady* smokescreen. Initials often denote someone who printed privately, or who was known in some other field, or who plain didn't want to be associated with *trade.* Anyway, I know the book you mean. It's reasonably rare, but not a phantom. I occasionally see copies."

"Is it still in print?" Pip asked. After all, herbals by John Gerard and Nicholas Culpeper were still reprinted, centuries after they were first produced.

"No. It's a nice book, but it falls through the cracks of being too modern to compete with the Big Two and also being a mix of scholarly information and old wives' tales. I think there may have been a single edition. What kind of order is yours in? Faded, you said?"

"Reading copy," Pip said. While that might have been a prevarication—she *must* stop doing that—it was technically true. It *could* be read and was therefore technically —

Oh, bother. Now I'll stub my toe or something. I should have said

62

Good.

"I don't want to sell it, anyway," Pip said.

"Fair enough." Jonquil sounded mildly disappointed. "What other old books do you have, Pippin?"

"Quite a few," Pip said vaguely. "You're welcome to come and see them if you're ever in my area."

"I'll hold you to that," Jonquil said. "Want to order any-thing today?"

"A dozen copies of *Grandmother's Sunshine*," Pip said evilly.

"Har-har." Jonquil laughed and hung up.

If only you knew . . .

Pip, having had her mind turned to old books, recalled her promise to get photographs of *The Apple Tree Prince* for Magda. She used her camera to take some. She was aware that her dedicated camera did a lesser job than Clarkia's phone, but that wasn't enough to remove her allegiance from her First-Generation Pink Princess. She carefully uploaded the pictures to her computer, cropped them, and sent them to Magda.

Maybe, she hoped, that belated promise-keeping might preserve her toes and fingers from the universe's punishment for fibbing — sort of — to Jonquil.

She shelved *Herbal Lore* by C C R with her other old books — she might want to consult it sometimes — and returned to the boxes.

CHAPTER ELEVEN. AMATEUR ACCLAIM

Over the next few days, Pip spent several pleasant hours speculating over old belongings she recalled and others she didn't, but ultimately, even with Clarkia's practical and modern-eyed assistance, she didn't find a lot to give away or to toss. Generations of the family had kept favourite items, but Pip realised they had been choosy regarding what they kept to express themselves to posterity.

Clarkia's spreadsheet detailed the treasures, and Pip, somewhat relieved, packed most of it away again.

She meant to be more ruthless with her own memorabilia, but as she and Clarkia unpacked plush cat after plush cat, she discovered her memory of a parade of identical stuffed toys was incorrect. Each was subtly different.

Clarkia did some research online. "Pip, I think these are *Kitty's Corner* cats."

"Ja. *Und?*"

"They were a companion line to the *Sirius's Star Dogs* range."

Pip made a winding motion with her fingers.

"Those were nineteenth century stuffed toys, all hand-made," Clarkia said. "There were lots of them, but the cats came out later, as a limited edition, all numbered. I think they might have been available by subscription, or maybe to existing Sirius customers."

Pip picked up the nearest plush cat. It had a crooked smirk, and its diamante collar glittered through its fur. Pip undid the collar and squinted.

"I need your mum's magnifying glass," she said to Clarkia.

"Just as well I have one too," Clarkia said, fishing it out of her hoodie and passing it to Pip.

Pip applied the magnifier to the collar. "It says *Camber 9.*"

"Check another one," Clarkia suggested.

Pip took up one with a longer tail. "Um . . . *Claudette 16.*"

"Well, well!" Clarkia said. "They're not in their original boxes, but according to the company website, these are worth quite a bit as collectors' items."

"Define quite a bit."

"That depends on who you're asking. A collection this size — are they all here?"

"All except the ones your mum forgot to give you — and one collar someone lost or kept when she borrowed the cat years ago. I have the cat — just not the collar."

"You should probably get them appraised," Clarkia said.

"Sometime. Maybe." Pip stared at the cats. They were mildly interesting, but really —

Not half so interesting as we are, Kittisack opined in smug Cat-Morse.

Pip checked names and numbers for Clarkia's spreadsheet and repackaged the cats, before unpacking a box of seed-pearl bracelets. They *were* practically identical, as she'd remembered, with the different enamel and gemstone dangles to make them individual.

Pip wondered if Biblio-Rep would like them for costumes. Or maybe she could think up a ballet . . . *Delphine's Children.*

She had just discovered a box of costumes and cuttings from her early days as a performer when someone tapped on the door.

Tell no one, Kittisack Cat-Morsed, puffing his whisker pads.

I shall be under the ivy, Amberjill added.

The cats slid out of sight.

Clarkia turned a little pale. "Pip, did they just . . . um . . ."

"Yes," Pip said. "They do that. Do you mind dealing with whoever it is, Clarkia? I'm a bit gummed up."

"What with?"

"Glue from my time as a fan dancer . . .unless it's left over from the decoupage. The feathers—"

"I'll get it," Clarkia said as the rap came again.

She went to the front door and Pip heard some distant conversation. She supposed it was one of Clarkia's friends, or possibly someone looking for directions, so she was surprised when Clarkia returned with some vaguely familiar people.

On her knees, with an armful of feathered fan and rather a lot of unreliable decades-old glue, Pip puzzled for a moment before recognising the young camerawoman with fair curly hair.

"Allirra?"

"Hi, Pip," Allirra Diamond said.

It took some sorting out, but it devolved that Allirra had come along with the presenters of the *Amateur Acclaim* documentary on the basis of her work with *Queen of the Clowder* and her acquaintance with Pip. She reintroduced the team she and Pip had met at the Forever Studios, and Clarkia dispatched herself hurriedly to *Jelly-and-Juice* where she used her staff discount to buy afternoon tea.

Pip surprised herself, and probably Clarkia, and definitely the sentient lemon tree by spending a few pleasurable hours talking ballet, plush cats, boxed-up memories, and the benefits of strawberries and cream.

The fact that it was the last day of June and she had expected the visitation on July 3 bothered her a bit until Allirra whispered she thought they'd mixed up the dates, which probably came of having a bunch of amateurs making a documentary. "We were *supposed* to come on the third, not the thirtieth—I think . . ."

A quick text to Magda confirmed this slip-up, rendering

everyone except Pip and Clarkia sheepish.

Magda loomed out of a follow-up video call made to Al-lirra's phone since Pip's First-Generation Pink Princess didn't know what video was. She suggested her client might ask for any footage to be scrapped and the filming done again on the correct date — or not at all.

Pip said on the whole she'd enjoyed herself, but not enough to want to do it all again. She was happy to be represented with a few feathers attached — though privately she was disappointed in not getting to wear her new dress from *Fairings*.

The small crew departed with the footage, apologies, resolutions to do better, and stomachs full of tarts. The crew, excluding Allirra, who was driving the camera, had even enjoyed an impromptu ballet lesson with Pip.

Clarkia looked doubtful of this enterprise, but Pip, who had got most of the glue off herself while demonstrating the queen's solo from *Queen of the Clowder*, repacked the plush cats — again — stacked up the clippings and costumes to be properly perused another time, and settled down to read the book Gillan St Ives had given her — *Orders of Field and Forest*.

She knew she should have read it before because it concerned fay animals.

Just too busy to focus, I suppose. Must do better.

And that was why she could so easily forgive the *Amateur Acclaim* film crew.

"Pip?" Clarkia's voice broke through her study of fay geese, some of which she'd encountered at the *Over Here B&B* where she'd stayed with Star Calder-Quince and some others when they went to the *Forever* gig.

"Hmm?" She glanced up and smiled thanks as Clarkia slid a cup of cambric tea onto the table beside her.

Clarkia was looking at her with an expression Pip thought was probably baffled interest.

"Hmm?" she said again, marking her place with a stray

feather.

"Has anyone ever told you—" Clarkia broke off. "Where are Kittisack and Amberjill?"

"Terrorising the plush cats in their crate, I think." Pip cocked her head. "Yes, I hear them rustling. What were you going to say?"

Clarkia smiled. "Never mind. Do you want me to add your costumes and cuttings to the spreadsheet?"

"Probably. Sometime." Pip returned to the fay geese.

Amberjill flitted across the room in pursuit of a lemon.

Chapter Twelve. Jellico Diamonds

Pip had a small collection of Jellico diamonds already. She'd found them on her walks along the beach and stored them in the dainty porcelain shoes she kept on the mantelpiece along with Lupin's cat, some empty beetles, and Little Pop Pearmain's shell-casing candlesticks.

One evening when Clarkia was out with a friend, Pip took down her three favourite porcelain slippers and emptied their glittering cargo onto the marigold-printed cloth Gillan St Ives had given her. She intended to do something special with that cloth, but she hadn't yet decided on what. It was far too wonderful to put in the bottom drawer and at her age there was little point in keeping it *for later*.

There were not a great many gems. She'd been combing the beach for a decade by now, and besides the one she'd found on her first childhood visit to the bay with Big Nanna de Leon, she'd picked up another twenty or so. Pip thought that was a good number. If the odd gems had been too common, she'd have lost interest in collecting them long ago. If they'd been too rare, she'd have become disheartened. As it was, the possibility of finding one on any given walk hovered between hope and possibility. She knew they weren't really diamonds, but some kind of topaz. Other people collected them, too, but Pip had no interest in comparing and contrasting her finds with someone else's. She hoped other people did find them, but their search had nothing to do with hers.

She picked them up in turn, rolling each one thoughtfully in her palm. She recalled finding almost all of them. Each held a shining memory of a sunny, blustery, chilly, golden, blue, or steel grey day. She'd found them at high tide, low tide, morning, noon and even, twice, under a moonlit magical sky. She hadn't gone to the trouble of walking backwards naked on those occasions, but she'd found them all the same.

What are you doing?

Amberjill had come in silently and pussyfooted up to startle Pip.

She reached out an inquisitive paw.

Choosing a gift for Alain. Maybe.

Pip didn't say it aloud.

Amberjill sniffed. *These have been washed in Lemon General.*

"It was necessary," Pip said. "I found some of them under heaps of that popping seaweed. They smelled far too fishy to keep in the cottage without a wash. Lemon General is good for cleaning almost anything."

Find him a new one, without fish, Amberjill advised.

Pip sighed. She didn't ask how Amberjill knew about Alain. She'd decided it was better for her psyche just to accept that the cats knew what they knew.

I would, but they're not something I can pick up every day. I might see one twice a year, if I'm lucky.

I can find one.

How?

I can find one, Amberjill repeated.

Pip didn't disbelieve her, and the idea was tempting, but where would be the fun in that?

She swept up the gems and poured them back into the shoes. "I'll go for a walk."

And if you find one, that will be the *one,* Amberjill suggested.

I don't expect I will.

Pip put on the riding boots Sulane had given her. They were by far the most forgiving shoes she had — as comfortable as her green ones with the daisy toes, but less inclined to let in sand and sea.

Pip worked to keep them supple with bucket oil made to old Mister Clancy's recipe. She didn't know if they really needed it, but it seemed the grateful thing to do. Besides, the bucket oil smelled agreeable.

She hummed as she left the garden of Lemonwood Cottage and strode along Ribston Lane treading on a private piece of her fairyland. She turned into Hope Street and followed it through the centre of town and out to Citron Parade, which sounded swish but which dwindled soon to little more than a sandy path leading down to the beach.

The smell of seaweed, salty air and the elusive acacia-like perfume of the winter-blooming Jellico citron wattle re-minded Pip briefly of *over there*. She shook off the yearning nostalgia and crunched down onto the beach.

The sand at the bay was white and fine, sparkling with scraps of shell. A band of seaweed and driftwood marked the tideline, and the wide sweep of the bay ran around to the promontory known locally as Jellico Rocks.

Humming, Pip strolled along, thinking of nothing in par-ticular. Her mind often went on autopilot when she walked along the beach. It was at once strange and familiar, like a painting which the artist subtly reworked every night and re-hung at dawn to confuse the household.

Surely that pink shell was there yesterday?
There's the cuttle bone under the log.
Is that a flute half-buried in the sand?

Pip went to see. It wasn't a flute—yet—but she saw how it might become one.

Dai Daffyd, the musical priest, played a brine flute which made a rueful, wistful, haunting sound reminiscent of de-serted merfolk kingdoms and ghost ships in the bay.

There was a story, somewhere, about a ghost ship in the bay. Her captain was doing penance, until a living girl told him he didn't have to.

Galleons, Pip thought. She wanted to sail on one. She

wanted to ride in a carriage and dance at a midnight ball with a man who smelled of toast. She wanted to go home with him under the stars and debrief in a room with a leaping fire. They'd be drinking something spicy, finishing one another's sentences, or keeping the lovely silence alive.

Doing any of those things seemed improbable for Pip.

But I'm so lucky. I have ballet and books, and friends and the cats . . . I'm so, so lucky.

She picked up the piece of driftwood and ran her fingers appreciatively over its silky flanks. She had no idea how to turn it into a flute, and her gluey venture into decoupage — she was halfway through her third jar, which was proving as incalcitrant and lumpy as the first and second — had reinforced her notion that she, like Cousin Lupin, but unlike Cousin Jan, was not crafty.

I'll give this to Dai if I see him again. He can make it into a flute or keep it as a souvenir of a place he's probably never been.

Pip dusted off sand and tucked the driftwood into her messenger bag. Something gleamed in the small damp depression left behind when she lifted the proto flute. Pip picked it up.

She had her Jellico diamond.

Just like that.

Pip looked around suspiciously, in case Amberjill had followed her, but the beach was innocent of little cat feet. Since she was pretty sure Amberjill had phasing talents, this didn't prove a lot, but Pip decided to take the win.

She pulled out the wisp of cloth she'd used to protect her ring of kindness before she took to wearing it every day. She wrapped her prize with care and put it safely away in the inner pocket of her messenger bag.

She continued her walk out to Jellico Rocks, then danced her way back across the sand.

She didn't have galleons, midnight balls, or carriages, but she always had her dancing.

CHAPTER THIRTEEN. BACK IN PRINT

G*randmother's Sunshine* was officially back in print. Pip and Clarkia received advance copies a full week before they were supposed to leave for *Tales in Tune*.

Jan had called, sounding excited, to gush over the beauty of the edition, so Pip slid hers out of the express post bag with high anticipation.

Her first impression was of a deep oddness.

She had lived with Cammie's copy of the book for decades. Years went by when she didn't open it, but it was settled in her mind as part of what made her what she was. She had shared knowledge of the stories and poems inside with her cousins, her mother and aunt, and Little Nanna Laurel. Nanna Pearmain had known them, but simply as stories she read to Pip.

Until recently, she had thought of it as a Laurel inheritance, but Clarkia's research, done years ago but only recently known to Pip, showed this was far from so. Schizanthus Laurel had been born Schizanthus Bay. Did that make it a *Bay* inheritance? Hardly, since Schizanthus had had it from *her* mother, who had been born a Godsell. It did Pip's head in.

She knew Clarkia was working anew on the family tree, but it was a slow proceeding. Most people who worked through the Link-Me website evidently pooled their work on different branches of the family, but so far Clarkia had failed to identify any other branch. She'd traced the generations patchily back to Cammie and Callie, whose grandmother had written their names in the books.

Callie's married name had been Calanthe Godsell, but her sister Cammie simply vanished from the fossil record.

As Clarkia said, "She might have married someone called John Smith and disappeared into a tangle of *Missus John Smiths*. Even old newspaper articles rarely mentioned women's first names. They were *Mrs Smith, Miss Smith,* or *Mrs John Smith.*"

"Not Miss Emeline Smith?"

"Um . . . occasionally. That usually meant a second or third daughter. As in *Miss Smith, Miss Emeline Smith* and *Miss Christina Smith.* The did use first names for births, weddings and death notices. *To Mr and Mrs J. Smith, a daughter, Emeline Rose.* Or sometimes, it's *To John Smith and his wife, a daughter, Emeline Rose.*"

Wherever Cammie had gone, she had not taken her book with her, because it had come down through Little Nanna Laurel and Little Mum to Pip.

Seeing the new edition, with the joint forward she, Jan, and Clarkia had written explaining as much as they knew of the provenance of the book, gave Pip a jolt. The book was so . . . *new.* The corners were so *cornery.* The cover was firm and slippery, and the pages were—her impression was that the book was slimmer, but she realised it was just the effect of the thinner paper. It was good quality paper, made with rag, but it was still undeniably modern.

Heirloom quality, was what the Unicorns said in *their* forward. *Timeless,* they'd added, suggesting the book could be shared across the generations. *Treasured,* they stated, which might be a unicornian explanation for the upmarket pricing that matched the upmarket production values.

This isn't it. It isn't right. It's not my Grandmother's Sunshine.

The thoughts clamoured through Pip's mind.

Then—ker-*ching*. Everything settled into place. The new

edition wasn't *her Grandmother's Sunshine.* It didn't have *To my darling Cammie, with love from Grandmother Aster* on the frontispiece. It wasn't *hers,* but it didn't need to be. She *had* hers.

This one could belong to Tamzin, and to Gillan, and to Music, and to Camelot and to Magda and to Jonquil, and to Mirri and to Soash . . . it could be *theirs* and each copy could be made uniquely *mine* for somebody. The Laurel-Bay-Godsell legacy could become a legacy for others — a sharing of the love that came from family.

Pip sighed happily.

She leafed through the edition with more attention, planning and smiling as she reacquainted herself with old friends. The forest lady. Tedwin from the castle. The waterfall children. The ageless pony from *The Gifted One.* The twins with the bucket of bulbs. The three cats. The goatherd. The riotous dogs. The sisters in the garden. The magic fiddle. The door in the chalk that led to the lovely lands. The island of change. They were all there, waiting for new readers.

Very old friends, Kittisack commented, flicking his tail.

"Hm?" Pip reached out to rub the original cat under his jaw. He smoothed his cheek across her fingers and added in his most sinister tone, *Tell no one.*

The bulk of the copies for the launch were travelling to Delphinium Island with Dirk Hendrik, the Hot Unicorn who was *not* expecting a baby.

He was leaving three days before the festival, giving him a chance to *set things in place,* as he put it.

Pip wondered what that meant. Presumably, he was trying to plan for a launch that would be running along with other unrelated books.

She packed for the festival with care. She always travelled light, and so did Clarkia, which meant they would each make do with one case and their cabin baggage. Pip's light packing was less light than usual because she had no idea of how long she'd be gone.

"You'll be seeing your pup the day we arrive though, won't you?" Clarkia said reasonably when Pip admitted her uncertainty. "Then meeting us at the festival that evening or the next morning?"

"Probably. That's the plan."

"There's the launch on the fifth day of the festival, and I expect we'll all stay on for the whole thing. Mum and Dirk *have* decided to launch *Garterstakes* as well, since there will be multiple launches, and—um—Dad's coming."

No! Pip's mind yelped. She barely knew Mark Sharman, and she'd been counting on a family outing with her only relatives.

Dear Mistress, this man is Clarkia's father. He is part of your family, Lupin's cat said gently.

Pip unclenched her hands. She got up to boil the kettle and took down her festival cup. Then she hung it up again and exchanged it for the marigold cup. She needed all the kindness she could muster.

"I hope he enjoys himself," she said.

Clarkia chuckled. "So do I! Poor Dad, he's more interested in football than festivals, but he said if Mum was launching a novel he *was* going to be there."

"Has he read it?" Pip asked.

"Um—no." Clarkia's shoulders shook with laughter. "Mum's going to provide him with a cheat sheet to use if anyone asks what it's about. Not that she's going to be there as Juniper Gin . . . Anyway, if we stay for the full festival, we'll still be gone no more than ten days or so."

"It might be longer for me," Pip admitted.

Clarkia looked as if she was going to enquire why, but visibly changed her mind. She and Pip had an unwritten agreement to stay out of one another's personal business.

Because Clarkia hadn't asked, Pip told her. "I may be

collecting a new bucket. And there's just a chance I might stay on to visit an old acting friend. We were in a film together when I was sixteen, and we met up again in April. He invited me to visit him at his manor, but we didn't make concrete arrangements."

"Manor? As in large house, or cockney stamping grounds?"

"I'm not exactly sure, but I think it's a country house. On an island."

"That sounds exclusive. Millionaire?"

"I shouldn't think so."

Clarkia said, "I see, but it shouldn't constitute a packing problem if you're going to be in a country house. I've noticed that you need practically as much luggage for three days as you do for a week, and whatever will do for a week will probably do for three or four, because you can wash it and just keep recycling pieces."

Especially if you live in leggings and oversize T-shirts and hoodies, Pip thought.

"Unless your friend lived in the tropics, or . . . or at a ski resort, or posh hotel or something like that, I mean. If he did, you'd need cool things or puffas and long johns or a dinner dress."

"Obviously I've never been there, but it doesn't sound snowy or tropical," Pip said. "He has horses."

"You'll probably need riding clothes then — unless they're racehorses."

That was easy enough. She had the riding outfit from Jane's sister, Sulane. That would do for everyday use if — or when — she went to Alain's manor. In the end, Pip took Clarkia's advice and packed two favourite shirts, her riding outfit, underthings and socks and, naturally, her sunrise dress. She elected to wear her vintage jeans and another favourite shirt.

She could always pick up additional clothing at the

festival.

At the last minute, she unhooked the extravagant marigold-printed cloth Gillan had given her from her bedpost and folded it into her bag.

One never knew when one might need a jolt of marigold splendour.

CHAPTER FOURTEEN. AT THE FOOT OF THE ESCALATOR

Pip stepped off the escalator in Sydney airport with Jan, her husband Mark, and Clarkia.

She was surprised to see Magda Saxer waiting for her.

"Ooh, look at that lush shawl!" Jan said audibly.

Pip bit her lip. Her agent was indeed a striking figure with her white milkmaid braid, her handsome features, and her fabulously embroidered wrapper, but Pip still didn't like it when her worlds collided.

It had been awkward enough when Jamie Pendennis arrived that morning to cat-and-cottage-sit and encountered the rest of the festival party.

Mark, with sandy hair going grey and wearing low-slung jeans and a polo-shirt, had greeted Jamie and asked jovially where his dog was.

Pip concluded that Jan must have mentioned that Pip's cat-sitter had a dog, possibly in relation to Pip's soon-to-be acquired pup. There was no reason for her not to speak of it, but it was awkward since Jamie couldn't produce Kakao for immediate inspection.

Fortunately, Jamie must have learned something since being grilled by Pip the first time he cat-sat, because he beamed at Mark and said he'd come directly from work to see if Miss Pearmain had any extra instructions for him, and that his dog would be joining the household later that day.

It was more or less true, Pip reflected. Undoubtedly Kakao

would be set loose, released, or manifested . . . maybe that was the preferred term . . . that day for the gratification of the lemon tree and the cats.

Jamie also volunteered to drive the party to the airport, which would save on parking fees, and to collect them on their return.

"That's generous of you, mate," Mark said, although Pip thought he looked a wee bit uneasy. Presumably a man in his sixties, having only recently given up on his high-powered motorcycle, did feel nervous of being driven by a very young man sporting P-plates.

His offer was accepted, though, so Pip got to have another ride in a Vouch-Safe vehicle. This time, at least, she knew where she was going. Jamie was an excellent driver — as well he might be with his fay perceptions and dedication to his job — and Mark visibly relaxed.

Now that Jan had spotted Magda at the airport, Pip felt obliged to perform more introductions.

"Magda, these are my cousins, Juniper and Clarkia, and Jan's husband, Mark Sharman," she said abruptly as they stepped off the escalator.

Magda offered her hand to Jan. "Magda Saxer. I'm Pippin's agent." She gave her a smile. "It's good to meet you, Missus Sharman. I understand it's down to your generosity as well as Pippin's that I'm to have prints from your delightful family treasure to display at my gallery."

"Jan's the one who arranged for the printing via publishers at Hot Unicorn Press, and Clarkia did some research to try to discover the provenance of the book," Pip said.

"I also have you to thank for sending photos of the book to Pippin initially so I could see them," Magda said to Clarkia.

She turned to Mark. "I hope you enjoy the festival, Mister Sharman. You're a brave man to venture forth. My husband loves me devotedly, but he declines to get, as he puts it, *entangled in mad creatives."*

"He's not creative?" Jan asked, with an amused glance at her husband that suggested that he wasn't, either.

"I wouldn't say that. He's very creative on the flugelhorn."

Mark's eyes lit up. "I've often wondered about those. I mean—how do you transport them."

Magda looked puzzled and glanced at Pip for enlightenment.

Pip shrugged.

Magda said, "Flugelhorns fit into cases, but alphorns, which Tork also plays, are a different matter. They come apart, but even so, the bits are long enough, especially the four-metre type. Tork, naturally, has the longest one he could contrive. I don't know *how* long, exactly, since he declines to tell me, but I'd say it's well over four metres. It's not a thing one could overlook in a taxi."

"I'd love to hear him play," Mark said.

Magda smiled. "Mister Sharman, I'll see what I can do. If I send him a message saying he might meet a fellow *hornliebha-ber*, I might be able to lure him to the festival after all."

"Horn lover?" Mark asked.

"That's it." Magda nodded approval.

"Ich habe Deutsch in der Schule gelernt," Mark said carefully.

"I did two years of French," Jan commented.

Pip, having known the cheesemaking Herr Fischer who was a good friend of Big Pop de Leon, decided Mark must mean he'd studied German at school. And he still remembered some of it! She wondered if he consciously kept in practice. She hadn't kept up her ballroom dancing—or her fencing, come to that, but she did practise her ballet.

Magda, having shown such unexpected tact for Mark, turned to Pip. "I understand you're not coming to the island immediately, Pippin?"

"No, I'm meeting a—" Pip hesitated. She couldn't claim

Gillan St Ives as a friend. They'd met just once, and it had been a prickly encounter. On the other hand, Gillan was doing her an enormous favour, so *acquaintance* didn't cut it. She tried another tack. "Someone who's going to take me to the breeder to choose my pup."

"In that case, would the rest of you care to travel with me?" Magda asked.

Pip gave her an enquiring glance.

"My friend Pandora Inkersoll—you remember her, Pippin—is driving down in a van. She is bringing some of her family's artwork to demonstrate *stories in pictures*. They're to provide a focus for one of the musical workshops."

Jan rolled her eyes sideways to Pip, who nodded. "Grand idea." Secretly, Pip thought Pandora would be relieved. Magda tended to bother Pandora regarding her refusal to accept Magda's old friend Peter P as her father. She was less likely to do so in a van full of humans. She added, "Thanks, Magda, and thank Pandora for me. I'll see you all either tonight or tomorrow. If you and Pandora want to share a cabin this time, I'm happy to bunk in with Clarkia."

Or maybe Pandora will make other plans.

With the travel arrangements made, Magda strode off, followed by the bemused-looking Sharmans.

Pip, standing at the base of the escalator with her messenger bag and her case, felt odd.

Being alone with the cats had been her default setting for a long while, but having Clarkia for an extended stay had gently reaccustomed her to the pleasures of living with someone else.

It had also brought her a pair of scissors and a rather good set of knives, not to say someone skilled at making soups and spreadsheets. If Clarkia missed her old life with her perfidious ex, she never mentioned it.

Pip shook herself mentally. The foot of an escalator was no place for tiny Pippin Pearmain to loiter. Someone might take her for a displaced karyatid and try to send her to lost luggage.

The sound of flights being called, people chatting and those airport buggies beeping started booming in her ears, so she headed for the exit. She should have walked with Magda and the others.

CHAPTER FIFTEEN. THE DOXIE OR THE SCOTTIE?

Once outside in the bright chill, she headed for an unoccupied seat in a *taxi only* zone and turned on her phone. She intended to call Gillan, or possibly to text her. That was the arrangement. She was about to do so when her phone woke with a glad chirp.

One new message.

Pip opened it with caution.

Miss Pearmain, my son will collect you from the airport and drive you to the Treadwells' guesthouse. I'll meet you there. As soon as you get this, send a message to my son to tell him where you are. This is his number.

Pip read that twice and typed a return to say she had arrived and would do as Gillan asked.

She was preparing to send it when a car drew up next to the seat and a young man stuck his head out the window.

"Pippin Pearmain?"

"Yes." She looked him over. He had delft blue eyes and dark hair. He was certainly one of Gillan's sons, but which one? They were close in age, looked alike, and were both muties who could turn into dogs.

"Are you the doxie or the Scottie?" she enquired.

"If you mean am I the one who observed you trying to converse with Lady Velvet in the Fairy Gardens . . . yes. I'm Zennor. Ma sent me because she thought you'd recognise me."

"I would have if I hadn't met your brother on the boom gate at the last festival. You are quite alike."

"We're brothers, so that's to be expected."

"My cousins were sisters, and they weren't a bit alike. Lupin was tall and elegant with dark hair until she went grey. Jan is sturdy and pink-cheeked with sandy-pepper-and-salt."

He seemed about to answer but must have thought better of it.

Pip frowned. "Are you supposed to be parked here, Master St Ives?"

"Of course not, so you'd better get in." The passenger door popped open.

"I have luggage."

He clicked his fingers. The case vanished and reappeared in the back seat of his car.

"Nice trick." Pip got in and did up her seatbelt. "I'm going to choose a puppy," she mentioned.

Zennor said, "That's what *you* think's going to happen."

"That's what *is* going to happen."

He pulled away of the airport and got onto the highway. "It's not. You most likely *are* going to get your pup, but you won't be doing the choosing. The pup will. Possibly the bitch will want some input, but generally they trust the pups."

"Oh. Okay. That makes sense." Pip settled back. She was quite pleased. She'd been wondering how she could choose from three possible pups. She would much rather be chosen than have to choose. To be chosen implied worthiness.

She did hope, however, that there wouldn't be too many choices available. What pup, for example, would choose her if there was a nice boy like Trae or a sensible girl like Sulane in the selection? Pups liked to play, and it was a long time since Pip had done that.

The drive to the guesthouse was brief, and a few minutes later, Zennor was opening the door again.

"Are you coming too?" Pip asked.

He shook his head. "I make the occasional dog nervous.

Most are fine with me, but now and again some aren't. I think they can sense Demi, but they can't quite work him out."

"On account of his being see-through?" Pip hadn't seen Zennor's insubstantial dachshund self, but she *had* heard of him.

"No. On account of his not being permanently present. Have you ever heard of one of those very short stories that pop up telling of disappearances or visitations or . . ." He waved a hand.

"Yes. Why?"

"Ever heard the one about someone following a set of hoof-marks through the snow then noting that they just stopped? Implying the one who made them went all *Beam me up Scotty* or possibly *springheeled like Jack*?"

"Um. Probably." Pip felt a twinge of unease.

"That's the way some dogs feel when they meet me — or rather, Demi. He's there — then he's not. Anyway, I'm not coming along to possibly disconcert a bitch or to trouble her pups."

"Your mum is coming though?" Since Gillan's other self was a black spaniel named Lady Velvet it seemed to Pip that she'd be just as disconcerting as her son.

"Yes, but she's a different matter. The breeder is an old friend of hers, and the dogs *know* her — and Lady Vee."

"I see. Well, when I get the pup I'll introduce him to your Demi. I want him to understand things like that."

Zen offered his hand, and Pip took it. "Thank you," he said. He added, "I'll leave your case in the car because I'll be driving you down to the festival later."

"That's kind of you," Pip said.

He shrugged. "No trouble. I'll be interested to know how you manage with the pup."

"So will I. Wish me luck."

"Luck," he said.

Pip said, abruptly, "You have a baby, don't you?"

He nodded, and his face lit up. "Camelot."

Camelot. Now she remembered. "Lovely name. I expect you call her Cammie."

"We do."

Pip let herself into the back seat, unclipped her case, and took out a book, which she handed to Zennor.

He took it, opened the cover and turned a few pages. "Mum buys a lot of books for Cammie and Madoc — that's her cousin — but I haven't seen this one before."

"Hardly anyone has — yet. It was my favourite book when I was a child. It belonged to my mother, and to her mother and so on, right back to an ancestor whose name was also *Cammie*, though probably not *Camelot*. Not this copy," she added quickly as she saw him testing the undeniably cornery corner with his thumb. "Mine is old. This one is a modern reprint." She added, "I'd like to give this copy to you for your Cammie."

"Thank you," he said. "Githa and I read to her every day, and this looks perfect."

"It's old-fashioned," Pip said, suddenly nervous. It was all very well to want to share her treasure with the world, but she didn't want it despised for its lack of inclusiveness and electronics.

Zennor laughed. "What do you think *we* are, Miss Pearmain? Half my relatives have never even seen a mobile phone! Not one that works, anyway."

Pip said, "By the way, this is an advance copy, so can you please refrain from showing it to people — other than your wife and daughter — until the launch?"

"Will do. Does anyone else have copies?"

"The publishers, Jan, Clarkia and me — and I sent a copy to Tamzin and one to Magda. As far as I know, that's all." She closed her case and glanced at the guesthouse. "Is your mum here?"

"Probably inside taking tea and parkin with Joan — no, here she is."

As he spoke, the guesthouse door opened and Gillan St Ives stepped out. She spotted Pip and Zennor and strode over to greet them. She was a tall, striking woman with dark hair threaded with silver. She wore dark leggings with a long jade-green sweater over the top, and her wrists jingled with silver bracelets. "Greetings, Miss Pearmain. Are you ready?"

Pip nodded. She held up her wrist with the promise blank bracelet Gillan had given her in April. "It's gone black, but Tane Pendennis said that was okay."

She knew the Pendennis family were somehow connected to the St Iveses, but she wasn't clear how. She assumed it was something to do with the fact that there were muties in both lines.

"Quite okay," Gillan said. She beckoned Pip through into the courtyard belonging to the guesthouse. "You're up to speed with how this works?"

"Yes. You open the gateway. I hold your hand, or your elbow or something, and we step through."

"That's it. We'll be *going*. Do you understand?"

"Yes. I'll remember not to let go of you, because otherwise we'll get separated and you'll have to come and find me. Or send someone else."

"Ah. Do I take it you *have* let go?"

"Yes. When Tane Pendennis took me to the fossmere I let go and he lost me."

"For heaven's sake!"

"It was quite okay. He sent Jane to find me. She's his daughter, in case you didn't know."

Gillan looked grimly amused. "I don't have a Jane, and my son has declined to come with us, so just hold on. You can close your eyes if it helps."

"I'll be okay. It was only that first time. Where are we go-ing?" She half-hoped it was somewhere near the fossmere.

Gillan said, "It's a place called Ankt de Veil."

As they walked to the rear of the courtyard, Pip tried, and failed, to work out the semantics of that.

"Don't bother," Gillan said. She reached out one hand to open the gateway. From this side, it looked like a small wooden gate leading through to a garden. Gillan added, "Holding hands would be better, if you don't object. It makes it less likely that we'll get parted."

"Okay." Pip took Gillan's left hand, aware of the multiplic-ity of silver rings.

Gillan said, "Ready?" and they stepped through into the now-familiar area near the castle.

CHAPTER SIXTEEN. SHADOWHONDEN

Gillan started walking, but not in the direction that would have led to the fossmere. After a few seconds, Pip felt the adjustment that meant they were *going*.

The beautiful scenery of *over there* blurred around her, but she kept her eyes open so as not to miss the moment when Ankt de Veil appeared around her.

"What exactly *is* Ankt de Veil?" she asked. "Is it a river valley or—" She broke off.

"It's a waterfall village with a sluice that runs a watermill," Gillan said. "We're going to Huis van Honden, where we'll meet the *hondvrouw*. Her name is Imke Apeldoorn."

Pip's feet stuttered, and Gillan's strong fingers closed more tightly. "Don't worry. There won't be a pop quiz on all that," Gillan said. "Mevrouw Apeldoorn knows you're human. In any case, she also knows my *kanaal toespraak* isn't strong. If you don't understand something, just say *Ik weet niet,* which is, more or less, I know not. Or maybe, just say *huh*? That's practically universal."

Pip decided Gillan was laughing at her. "I take it she's kanaalfee," she said.

"Ye-es."

"You don't sound certain."

"Frankly, I'm not. The kanaalfee tend to live in small, isolated groups and they're so traditional you'd think they did it on purpose. Think round red cheese, think windmills, think clogs, think canals, think cows, think tulips . . . think chocolate. They're far more Dutch than the actual Dutch. However,

Imke is so involved in her vocation of raising fay dogs that she seems — I hesitate to say unique, but she *is*. And she has red hair and a penchant for bagpipes, so possibly there's a sporran of braesider in her blood — never mind. You're not going to be visiting often, so don't trouble yourself." She squeezed Pip's hand again. "Another few steps and we're there. Okay?"

"Okay." Pip counted down mentally from ten, but as she got to three, Gillan stopped and Pip lurched and almost fell over.

"Oops. Sorry."

"I'm fine." Pip looked around with interest, although she was aware Gillan hadn't explained what she had to do to impress a shadowhond and her pups. Maybe that was deliberate.

They'd come to a halt outside a large stone house. *Huis van Honden*, presumably.

It was one storey, but four or five times the size of Pip's cottage. Her vision of a cosy log fire with a bitch on a blanket with her pups around her, or possibly of a comfy stable with pups in the hay evaporated.

The house was surrounded by a large and productive garden, which softened the impression of dourness. A few paperwhites bloomed in the shelter of a wall, and the familiar pink and green and purple of hellebore, the Lenten rose, massed over a full bed. Wallflowers scented the air. Behind these Pip noted beds of kale and cabbages.

Gillan led the way along a winding path to the three steps leading to the door. She indicated the knocker, shaped like a running hound.

"Three taps, and after that probably you'll want to step back and to the side. This might be a bit disconcerting."

"As disconcerting as meeting Joan-troll and Trollie?"

Gillan chuckled. "I heard what happened. Joan said you

hardly turned a hair."

That wasn't how Pip remembered it, but she took the win and smiled.

"Knocker," Gillan reminded.

Hush you. Pip managed not to say it aloud. She looked at the knocker doubtfully, hoping she could reach it. She rose en pointe and got a grasp before giving the hound three good raps against the door.

Then, as Gillan recommended, she stepped back and to the side.

She heard the pattering of paws and turned to look at Gillan just in time to see the woman vanish. Her place was taken by a black spaniel bitch with a cool and superior expression.

Lady Velvet.

Gillan's dog self was handsome, just as her woman-self was, but when Pip had encountered her at the Fairy Gardens she had been annoyed and unresponsive. Gillan had apologised for her other self's attitude. Pip had no idea how Lady Velvet felt. As she had gathered that the two were quite separate entities, she thought it politic to greet the spaniel. She was trying to formulate something better than *hey, you!* to get the bitch's attention when what appeared to be a wave of thick black smoke poured through the wooden panels of the door.

Her ears felt odd, as if there had been a silent percussion or explosion, and she leaped back in automatic self-preservation.

The smoke flowed over the ground at knee-height and coalesced into a veritable river of dogs. The leader was a medium-sized dark-coloured dog with coppery tints to its ears and brows. The others were black and grey, with coats ranging from cut-velvet to shaggy, and long, sweeping tails.

They milled around the leader, sniffing and playing but unusually quiet.

Lady Velvet uttered a sound between a yip and a whine.

The copper-eared dog snapped its attention to the spaniel, and the two sniffed noses. Lady Velvet was the larger of the two, but she lay down, so her head was lower than the other's.

She's showing modified submission. If she was fully submitting she'd be rolling over.

Pip watched, fascinated as the copper-eared dog in turn lowered itself to a sitting position, making her eye to eye with the spaniel.

After a few seconds, the two rose to their feet, shook themselves and morphed into Gillan and a young woman who looked, to Pip's amazed eyes, to be no more than twenty-five.

She was tall and full-figured with a riot of red hair and a fair, freckled complexion. She wore a long pinafore dress over a heavy cream blouse, thick knitted stockings, and painted clogs.

Laughing, she turned to Pip, slapping her knees. "Good morning, Miss Pearmain. I apologise for the wanton display just now, but Tulp Anke sensed another mutie and as you see — " She turned her hands out. "She *would* manifest."

"You might have warned me," Pip said to Gillan.

"She might, but I asked her not to," the other woman said.

"Imke wanted to see how you reacted, I expect," Gillan said.

"What, to you playing one-up-bitchship? Oops . . . sorry. You weren't, were you? You were establishing equality."

The young woman grinned. "We were! You know something of dogs, then."

"More than I did," Pip said cautiously. "I've read up a few dog books, and also the *Orders of Field and Forest,* although that didn't say much about shadowhonden. If that's the right plural."

She looked around at the dogs, which were still sitting at attention. "May I?"

"Certainly." Imke Apeldoorn and Gillan moved aside and fell into conversation.

Pip, aware they were probably judging her out of the corners of their eyes, moved slowly towards the dogs. Tails thudded silently, and some of them raised paws to her.

Am I expected to shake?

She tried it out, gently grasping an offered paw. The dog looked her in the eye and allowed her to shake. She offered her hand to others, and some of them pushed up to her to have their ears rubbed.

Pip settled on the path, and the dogs crowded round, still silent.

You're a handsome lot. She used what she thought of as the Cat-Morse channel. It hadn't worked in the Fairy Gardens, but she felt an electricity in the air, as if something had connected.

Hondenpak wij. The odd words came in a kind of whispering chorus, making Pip's neck prickle.

Hondenpak. She knew honden meant *dogs,* so possibly they were referring to their group or pack?

She groped for a way to respond and came up with what Gillan had suggested.

She began, "Ik weet—" and broke off. She *did* know. She said, more certainly, "Hondenpak you . . . Ik weet."

She felt their tolerant amusement.

"All right, you lot. You've had your fun. You do Dog-Morse."

Hondenpak wij. Hond pak je.

Black noses nudged her. Pip rubbed ears and necks. Tails waved. The shadowhonden signalled acceptance. They might be silent creatures who could smoke their way through closed doors, but they were still dogs.

One dog pushed to the front. She was the palest Pip had seen, a misty shade of grey with silver eyes.

Pip stroked her and noted she'd recently had pups. She took a leap of faith. "Are you Maanlicht?"

Ik ben Maanlicht.

"Moonlight? I'm Pippin."

The bitch waved her tail. It would do. She took Pip's wrist, the one with the promise blank bracelet, gently in her mouth and tugged. *Kom Pepijn.*

That was clear, anyway. Pip got up, gently disengaging from Moonlight's jaws. The dog nudged her towards the door.

Pip glanced at Gillan and Imke. Imke waved a casual hand. "You go in. We'll follow in a bit."

CHAPTER SEVENTEEN. TEKTITE

Pip turned her attention to Moonlight, who pressed against her leg. Another dog came up on the other side. He was taller, and so black his coat seemed to swallow the light.

Stilte, he announced.

"That's your name?"

Ik ben Stilte.

The two dogs crowded her closer to the door. Pip felt suddenly uneasy.

Het is goed.

She found that if she listened with her mind, the signals made more sense. *It is good.* She'd have to take their word for it.

She raised a hand to open the door, but they suggested she should leave it to them.

Step on.

Pip closed her eyes and took a step, and another.

She was inside the house.

Well, you knew these dogs were schemers. Phasers. Or whatever.

Moonlight and Stilte, whose name seemed to mean *Silence,* urged her on along corridors and into a warm room where the winter sunlight flooded the paved floor. A large basket occupied the space near the window. In it slept four pups.

Pip saw now what Gillen had meant when she'd written that the pups were cherry, ash, charcoal and obsidian. Although they were snuggled together in a double yin-yang, the demarcation lines were clear. One had a short pelt of dark fur with a faint cast of dark red, the very colour of a black cherry.

The others were a light grey, just a few shades darker than Moonlight, a darker grey, and a glossy black who was the same colour as his father.

Pip eyed them eagerly. She itched to pick them up, but Zennor had told her the choice wasn't hers to make.

She turned to Moonlight and Silence. "These are your pups? They are beautiful."

Ours. Maybe you.

She wished they would be more explicit, but though she'd been Cat-Morsing with Kittisack for a long time now, this was new.

Kittisack! The dogs exchanged gleeful dog-grins. *He originele kat.*

Ja and groot annoying.

"You know Kittisack?"

Wij weet.

Moonlight went to the basket and thrust her nose in among the pups. *Wake you! Pepijn kom.*

The cherry pup opened blue eyes and yawned before curling back into sleep. The other three, the dog pups, stretched, flicked their stubby little tails and waddled to the edge of the basket.

Silence gave each one a good-natured nudge with his snout and they tumbled onto the floor, rolling like fat toys.

Pip, with her heart warming, slowly sat on the floor. *May I?*

Nee.

Her disappointment was bitter, but then she realised what Moonlight probably meant. The pups were to choose. She sat quietly, hands in lap, waiting and hoping. She couldn't help reaching out to the pups and found their baby minds full of thoughts of *basket, milk, warm, love, fun, play.*

They got up and had a brief tussle, uttering shrill growls. The darkest pup, secretly Pip's favourite, rolled out of the scrum and fetched up against her knees.

He sneezed, looking up at her with slatey eyes.

"Hello," Pip said softly.

He lifted one front paw and scratched at her leg with tiny claws. When she didn't respond, he tried to climb up, so she felt obliged to help him.

Bedankt.

Pip stroked the round little skull with one finger. Had the pup just thanked her?

He squirmed around and made himself comfortable. The other pups tumbled back to the basket.

Moonlight and Silence seemed to confer. Then Moonlight climbed into the basket and Silence left the room.

Pip stayed where she was, cradling baby Tektite in her lap. The pup had chosen *her*. He was the perfect bearer for the name she'd picked out.

She was lost in a happy dream when Imke and Gillan came in with Silence.

"All went well, I see," Imke said.

"He picked me." She felt proud and humble all at once.

Gillan glanced over the remaining pups. "They're growing up so fast."

Imke nodded. "They do." She indicated the cherry female. "Robijn is staying to join the pack. I have folk coming to see the others in a week or so."

"Not Tektite," Pip said jealously.

Imke said, "They will see him, but he has chosen. He will not leave the basket." She smiled, and added, "But for now, he should be with his mother, nee? She has more to teach him."

Pip nodded reluctantly. Already the small warm weight in her lap was *hers,* and he'd got into her heart. She glanced at the promise blank. It was no longer a generic pup. It was now undeniably a portrait of Tektite.

Gillan said, "It will be interesting to see if your Dog-Morse idea has any validity, Miss Pearmain."

"Pip."

"Pip, then. Even if it doesn't work the way you hope, you'll have a charming companion. Shadows are loyal."

"And discreet," Imke said.

Pip wondered what that meant. Moonlight and Silence had been pretty much obtrusive. She almost said her Dog-Morse was already working, but she held back. Time enough to explain to Gillan when Tektite was at home with her, exploring the cottage and the garden, probably bothering the cats and peeing on the sentient lemon.

Though that might take a while.

She was pretty sure it took weeks or even months before a boy pup could cock his little hind leg.

She might be able to take him to the fossmere to meet the family there, although she had no idea if he would be able to travel on a plane.

He must, though, if he was to get to Jellico Bay.

Still holding her new and treasured companion, she looked up at Imke. "Can you please let Gillan know when he can come to me? I can fly over to fetch him." She frowned. Dogs and cats didn't get to travel in the cabins of planes. They were transported in the hold. It was all proper and safe, she understood, but she had a fair idea of what Kittisack and Amberjill might have to say in response if she suggested they should fly to Sydney with her.

It *wouldn't* be *Tell no one.*

Gillan glanced at Imke. "I'm sure something can be arranged."

"Let me know," Pip insisted. "Don't just pack him in a crate or something."

"We'd never do that," Gillan soothed.

"Maybe—"

"It will be all right," Imke said. "He is a shadowhond from an ancient line."

Gillan said, "Is there much about them in *Orders of Field and*

Forest?"

"Not shadowhonden. Just a chapter on fay dogs in general."

"Really, I thought—I don't suppose you have a copy of it, Imke? It's a new book and I know you don't often go *over there.*"

The hondvrouw shook her head.

"I have mine with me," Pip said, dropping her hand to her messenger bag. She slid her fingers under the flap and pulled out the book. "I have read quite a lot of it, but somehow—" She broke off.

"Life has been busy," Gillan said, as if she knew what that was like.

"I've been sorting out crates and things. I read the chapters on fay cats, fay dogs, fay geese and goats and hill ponies, but I haven't really looked at the birds and cows yet." She handed the book to Gillan who took it and leafed through the pages to the section on fay dogs.

Gillan looked it over and frowned. "I see what you mean. I could have sworn—" She flipped to the back to look at the index. "Ah! It's not in the main fay dog entry at all. It's in the morphable section in the appendix, along with the phasers and the cloud-steppers. How peculiar." She handed the book back to Pip. "Maybe you can finish reading it before you take Tektite into your home. Or maybe those fay cats of yours can explain things to you."

Imke made an enquiring sound and Gillan said, "They really do communicate with Miss Pearmain, at least in some degree."

He will know, Moonlight commented. She glanced at Pip. *He needs milk.*

"Oh." Pip got carefully to her feet. For the benefit of the women, she said, "I suppose I'd better put Tektite back in the basket so he can get some lunch before the others drink it all." She dropped a kiss on the pup's head and gently restored him to his siblings. "I might be able to see him again in a few days . . . or maybe a couple of weeks . . . before I fly home. That's if Gillan doesn't mind piloting me."

Gillan said, "Let me know. I'd like to see these pups again. One of them might even choose me."

Imke said, "If you are serious, I'm sure Maanlicht would commend you to the ash and the charcoal."

"You don't name them?" Gillan asked.

Imke shook her head. "Shadow litters always come in different colour grades, so I refer to them by those. That way the name is chosen as a symbol of the bond between hond and companion." She turned her attention to Pip. "Tektite is a good name for the obsidian. A strong name."

Gillan said, "It's like naming a child. We puzzled for a long while before we named Mullion, but when it was Zennor's turn, we were so frazzled we let Mull stick his finger on the map." She sighed in a theatrical fashion. "And yet, it's been pointed out that Zen is the one whose name is more user-friendly. We completely overlooked the short form when we were naming Mull. Made a proper *mull* of that one."

"But it's also a promontory, a consideration verb, and a hot drink," Pip said.

Imke slapped her knees and laughed. "She got you on that one, Gillan."

The comment on Zen had reminded Pip of something. "I told Zennor I'd introduce Tektite to him sometime, so he'll understand different dog-selves. *I* don't have one." She glanced back at the little family. *Goodbye for now, Tektite. And Moonlight*, bedankt.

CHAPTER EIGHTEEN. CONVERSATION WITH THE CATS

Pip couldn't wait to describe the shadowhonden to the cats. She remembered telephoning Clarkia and Jan and conversing with Kittisack and Amberjill a few weeks before. It seemed bizarre that she could talk to cats on a mobile phone, but the idea of talking to cats was bizarre in any case.

Zennor collected her from the guesthouse and drove her down to Delphinium Island. She thought that was going way beyond the bounds of favours on such a slight acquaintance, but he said he was going to the festival anyway, taking his turn on the boom gate to check declarations. He reminded Pip that not only was he Tamzin Campania's foster brother, but also that he and his brother ran the dance club *Lanners*, and so were involved in the music industry.

In return, Pip told him a bit about the shadowhonden and reiterated her offer to introduce him to Tektite.

It occurred to her that he was one of the few people she knew, albeit slightly, who would accept dogs that phased into smoke form without a mental reservation. She almost mentioned Gillan's interest in possibly acquiring a pup, but that was none of her business, and probably none of Zen's either.

"I read some of the book while I was waiting for you," he said.

"Ja. *Und?*"

He flicked her a sideways glance. "What is that?"

"Cod German. Big Pop de Leon had a friend called Herr

Fischer. At least, I expect he had a first name, but *we* didn't know it. Big Pop called him *Hi.*"

"Heinrich, I expect," Zen said.

"Ja! Sehr gut!"

"Du sprichst Deutch?"

"Nein. Nee. Not at all."

"Didn't do languages at school?"

Pip chuckled. "My schooling was patchy because I was often working. As for language and what they used to call *accomplishments,* I learned what I needed for films and plays and things. I did pick up a few words of German from Herr Fischer, but it's not much use for normal conversation. I can recite a long list of German cheeses and sing *Margrete mein Leben* with the original lyrics. I picked up a few more words from Hein Hoffmann — he played the romantic lead in *The House of Heriot.*" She frowned, thinking of the Dog-Morse she'd absorbed from the shadowhonden. That hadn't been German, or even Dutch. Not proper Dutch. *Pidgin Dutch at best.* And yet she'd come to understand at least some of it.

"I might have been quite good at languages, maybe, if I'd ever learned any seriously," she said. She decided to ask the cats if they knew of any correlation between Cat-Morse and a latent ability with human languages.

It occurred to her that once she got to the festival it might be difficult to make a private phone call to cats, whereas now she had an hour or so in a car with just one other person — or two if she counted the insubstantial and currently invisible Demi.

"Zen, can you keep a secret?"

He glanced at her. "That depends. I can keep secrets if they're not harmful. I don't suppose your possible fluency in German cheeses is harmful. It's interesting. I do think the odd things people know are interesting."

"*No harm,*" she assured him. "And it's nothing to do with

cheese. Or not directly."

"In that case, you can tell me, if you want to."

"It's not something I want to *tell* you. It's something I want to do now. I can't prevent you from knowing, but I'd prefer you not to discuss it with anyone else because it sounds mad out of context. And people already think I'm as daft as a brush."

"That sounds a bit—odd."

Pip sighed, recalling Gerry Trip's caution about letting her contact Jamie.

Obviously, lovely lads needed to be protected from possibly predatory older women, but she did wish folk weren't so suspicious. Anyway, Zennor was older than Jamie, although probably not as old as Zach Rowan. He couldn't be branded as a *lovely lad*. Not with a wife.

Before she tangled herself more in explanations, she said, "*No harm*, honestly. I just want to make a phone call to the cats I live with. I'd like to do it now. I expect you'll think it's weird, or hilarious, or something, so I would rather you don't tell people. That's all."

She thought he'd agree, but he gave her a mischievous glance. "Not even Githa? We *are* one flesh and all that."

"You can tell Githa, but no one else." She remembered the lovely fair girl with the baby.

"Not even Guinevere?"

"Who is—oh, never mind. Not even. No. No one. Not that I can stop you."

"I won't tell."

He said nothing more, so Pip took out her phone and hit Jamie's number.

He picked up on the fourth ring. "Hello?"

"Jamie, it's Pippin Pearmain. Where are you?"

"Um—paying my rent to the lemon tree. I think it's starting to like me."

"Excellent. Are the cats there?"

There was an infinitesimal pause and she pictured him glancing here and there before he said, "Kittisack is . . . Not sure. Amberjill—oh, I see her—taunting the gooseberry bush."

Pip could just picture that. Amberjill was as light and unpredictable as a leaf in the wind, and she enjoyed playing her version of chicken with the spiny plant.

"Good. When you've finished paying your rent and zipped up, can you tell the cats I have news?"

"Sure. Just a sec." Pip heard him hailing the cats and thought anew what an obliging young man he was. It was a pity he wasn't older, or that Clarkia wasn't younger. She'd have liked to have him in the family.

"Okay. Cats' ears at the ready. Do you want me to tune out? I can prop the phone up and retreat to the kitchen."

Pip hesitated. She'd learned a thing or so of fay hearing. Jamie was a halfling, but she supposed he was probably pretty good in the ear department, having an inner dog.

"Never mind that. Listen or not. Just don't—"

"Repeat it. I won't."

Pip stuck her thumb in the air, though he wouldn't see it. "That's the proper response," she said to Zen.

"I beg your pardon?" Jamie sounded puzzled.

"I was talking to Zen. Zennor St Ives. Some kind of cousin of yours, I think . . . Is that right, Zen?"

"Since I don't know who you're talking to, I couldn't say. But, as he sounds obliging, he probably isn't a pisky and so not a very close relative."

"Jamie Pendennis. A quarter pisky, I think he said." Pip held up the phone. "Say hi to Zen, Jamie."

"Hi to Zen."

"Hi to you too, young Pendennis." Zen sounded amused. "How are you related to Merryn Pendennis, the jeweller at

Treborrow?"

"He's my pisky grandad. My hob grandad is Jem Cott-man."

"In that case, you are some sort of cousin, but we'd need a leppy gossoon to explain just where you fit in the tree. Just one more thing, are you — er — very like your pisky grandad?"

"No." Jamie sounded regretful. "I don't clank and chingle when I walk, and women don't stare at me and brighten up. I'm not a jeweller. I also don't hug everyone I meet and light up the room. I'm like him in one way though."

"Oh?"

Silence.

Pip said, "For heavens' sake, you two. Stop pussyfooting around. Jamie, he wants to know if you're a mutie like him."

"Oh! Yes. I have Kakao. Kind of a chocolate poodle."

"Demi-dog. Kind of a see-through doxie."

"Wow! That's different."

"If you've quite finished detailing your inner dogs, I'd like to talk to the cats," Pip said meanly.

"Yes ma'am."

Silence.

"Kittisack? Amberjill? Lupin's cat?"

She felt their awareness.

Did you meet our little dog? Amberjill wanted to know.

Pip decided to ignore the pronoun. After all, she had asked for their approval.

"I did, and he's perfect. He's very black and he *chose* me."

It was well done, dear mistress, Lupin's cat said.

"His mother is called Moonlight and his father is Silence. He can already —"

Does he use Cat-Morse? Kittisack enquired.

Pip slipped into mental response. She thought Zennor might not be proof against grilling by Gillan. *He used Dog-Morse, but only a wee bit. The other shadowhonden spoke to me.*

The way we do? Amberjill asked.

Not exactly. It was in a kind of pidgin Dutch, or kanaalfee speech, but I understood some of it.

We have trained you well, Kittisack said. He added quickly, *Tell no one.*

You have, Pip agreed, giving them fair credit. She could barely remember when she began to use Cat-Morse, or who had instigated it. It had to be either herself or Kittisack, because Amberjill had come later and Lupin's cat later still.

Tell no one. Kittisack sounded emphatic.

Why not?

Pip almost threw up her hands. She was nearly sure Kittisack was playing with her. Why on earth did it matter if she told someone?

"Tektite would want you to have cheese," she said aloud for Jamie's benefit. "Please ask Jamie to get you some from the pantry. I have a nice cheddar ripening in muslin."

The last word was barely out of her mouth when she had an impression of fleeting paws.

Jamie said, "I don't know if you realise, but the cats just took off. I think it was the C-word."

Pip thought it was too.

"Thanks, Jamie. You'd better let them have some. You and Kakao too, naturally."

"Thank you," Jamie said.

Lupin's cat, is everything all right?

All is well, dear mistress. Jamie is caring for my children.

Goodbye then. Thank you.

"I'd better go," Jamie said. "Is that all, Miss Pearmain?"

"That's all for now, Jamie. Goodbye."

Pip hung up. She glanced at Zennor's handsome profile. "You get thirty seconds to laugh and that's your lot."

"I'm not laughing."

"Oh?"

"No." He frowned. "What was with the long silence?"

"We went dark. Silent mode."

"Why not just run the whole communication that way?"

"I had to talk aloud to Jamie. *He* doesn't do Cat-Morse."

"I'm glad to hear it. My relatives are quite peculiar enough as it is."

"You don't actually know him, do you?"

"No. I know his line, vaguely. His father — well, I expect he's his father — is a mathematical prodigy. I take it Jamie is not."

"Are you fishing?"

He glanced at her again. "Not exactly. It's more genuine concern for the lad. It sounds as if his father and grandfather Pendennis are what you might call hard acts to follow."

"Maybe. I've met his grandfather, and he's certainly memorable. He made the bracelet I'm wearing. His uncle is also highly memorable — and half waterfolk. But you needn't be bothered for Jamie. He's a lovely lad, you see. And lovely lads do well because people like them and want them to be happy."

He was still frowning.

"What? What are you not saying?"

"Do you know my dad?"

"No, but I know your mum."

"Ma's a fullblood pisky minx. Dad's . . . well, just a tad over a halfling. The other half is human."

"So?" Jane Pendennis was a mixture of orders, and she said she relished the freedom of not having to conform to any expectations.

"Dad has always felt ever-so-fortunate that Ma chose to wed him. On account of having so much human blood. Nothing against humans! Definitely. Any other dilution would have been the same. However . . . Ma wanted to keep the mutie blood high in her line. Dad's not a mutie, but he's from a mutie strain which includes your Jamie. Anyway, Dad has become more successful and more determinedly *pisky* as he gets older. To make Ma never regret taking him on. If you know what I mean."

"That's ridiculous."

"I agree. Or rather, I would if not for feeling a shadow of the same myself. My Githa is a fullblood."

"And you feel ever-so-fortunate?"

"It's not the same. Dad and Ma sort of auditioned one another. Very businesslike. They were both looking to wed and start a family, and they made a pact and . . ." He waved one expressive silver-ringed hand. "It's been a most successful marriage. They truly love and respect one another. They *like* one another, which might be even more important. They laugh at the same things."

"But your dad feels *ever-so-fortunate.*"

"Yes. With Githa and me, it was different. Dahlia, who is our accountant and a family friend, invited her cousin Morgana to stay. Morgana brought Githa along. They were flatmates overseas. Morgana is not a mutie, but Githa is. I suspect it was *expected* that Githa and my brother Mull might connect. He's the Scottie, as you put it."

"Ja. *Und?*"

He gestured again. Pip wished he'd keep both hands on the wheel, although she suspected he could drive the car no-hands or standing on his head.

"Githa picked *me.* It wasn't just that. She didn't even notice Mull. She noticed *me.*"

"Why wouldn't she? You're—" Pip hesitated. Could even an *older woman* go around telling young men they were attractive? She decided one could. He was fay, after all, and the fay she'd encountered were all rather frank—when they weren't being devious. "You're good-looking and you smell nice."

"She picked *me.* Over all the full pisky men. Over my brother, who manifests a solid dog-self."

"And you picked her. Over all—" Pip broke off. *Oh.* She

said hurriedly, "So, Githa has a dog self too."

"Guinevere. The most beautiful little fairy hound you ever saw."

"And how does she get along with . . . um . . . Demi-dog?"

Zennor sighed. "Need you ask? He melts into a little puddle of adoration."

"And she?"

"She snuggles up with him and even manages to groom him. His consequence has improved a hundredfold at having his own hound to love."

"Then I can't see what the problem is. Or even *if* there's a problem. Stop analysing. You're not inferior. She's not superior. So, you have some human blood. It can't be *typical* human blood."

"Why do you say that?"

"Whoever it was fell in love with a fairy! And you and your wife can do a big favour to your little girl by making sure she knows that having a bit of atypical human blood makes her interesting. Not special. Not better or worse. Interesting. To be interesting is a great gift."

He seemed disconcerted, so she changed the subject. "You were saying you'd read some of the stories in *Grandmother's Sunshine* while you waited for me."

He switched tracks smoothly. The fay seemed good at that.

"I did. And you're right when you say they're old-fashioned. They're not wholly so, though. Often old-fashioned stories were highly didactic. These are simply stories of people, and creatures—there's no implicit reward for good behaviour and no hobby-horse being ridden. I'm looking forward to reading more, and to sharing them with our Cammie . . . and with Githa. May I ask which is your favourite?"

Pip had chosen one when it was time to write the dedication, so she had the answer ready. "I always liked the verses best. There's the kitten-cat rhyme . . . There's a dog rhyme,

too. I especially liked it that the rhymes have pictures just as detailed as the longer stories. Juniper — my cousin — liked — "
Pip broke off as her phone, which she was still holding, rang. She glanced down at it, thinking Jamie might have rung back, but the ID said it was Xavier Partridge.

"I'd better take this," she said.

Zennor nodded.

Chapter Nineteen. The Ultimate Bucket

"Miss Pearmain?" Xavier Partridge's voice sounded doubtful.

"Yes! Have you got my bucket?"

"I have. If you nominate a time —"

"Now! Where are you?"

"At home, but we can meet at the Fairy Gardens again if you like."

"Just a minute." Pip put her hand over the speaker. She didn't know why she bothered. Zennor and Xavier probably both had better than twenty-twenty hearing, or whatever the term was. She said, "Zennor, would you mind a quick diversion to the Fairy Gardens? I'm sure you know the way."

"I can do that."

Pip remembered her manners. "If it's awkward, you can drop me somewhere and I can get a taxi."

"Ma would have my hide. We can turn off and circle back."

Pip started to hum. She felt absurdly excited. A puppy and a superior bucket on the same day!

The phone quacked anxiously. Pip recalled the line was still active. She broke off her humming to say, "That's okay. We'll be there soon."

Zennor said, "Who are we meeting at the Fairy Gardens and why is he bringing a bucket?"

Pip explained.

He nodded. "He does good work. He made cradles for

Cammie and Madoc—and for Music, Tamzin and Matin's baby."

"Do you *all* know one another?"

"How do you mean?"

"I met Jamie sort of by chance when my cousin left me a V-S voucher and he turned up to drive me to meet a yacht called *Tulpenmanie*. His boss, or supervisor, or whatever, is called Gerry Trip. At the festival back in April, I met Jamie's sister and her friend Amaryllis, who is Gerry Trip's daughter. I met a woman named Jisinia on the yacht. Later I met a man who danced the male lead in my ballet. He's Jisinia's brother. I met their dad at a guesthouse. I met you and your mother in the Fairy Gardens, and now *you* know the man who carved me a bucket, and you're related to Jamie."

"Distantly. As in fourth cousin, or something. And yes, I suppose it is odd looking in from outside, but we do tend to know one another. We know plenty of humans too, but—"

"But I suppose you can relax more around other fay."

He shrugged. "Maybe. Remember, I have a reasonable percentage of human blood through my grandma's family, so I tend to feel okay with all sorts."

Pip said, "It ought to work like that, being with other performers, but it doesn't always."

"There you are, then. Are you looking forward to the premiere?"

"What premiere?"

"*Half-Life of the Lost*. It's being screened on Day Nine."

Pip wondered if she was supposed to have known that. "Oh. I suppose so. Yes, should be interesting."

Zenner pulled up opposite the tall statues. "The Fairy Gardens," he announced, unnecessarily. "And there, I assume, is your bucket."

Pip perceived that the dark-haired elf man was back. This time, he was leaning against a tree, eating a tart.

Beside him was a large crate.

"Want me to come?" Zennor asked.

"If you like." Pip got out of the car. "Master Partridge."

"Miss Pearmain," he responded. "You're wearing pink."

Pip glanced down at herself. She had worn her favourite vintage flared jeans and a pink and green checked shirt with a pink rose on the pocket for puppy visiting. "I like pink."

He indicated the crate. "Here's the bucket. Why have you brought a pisky?"

"I didn't *bring* a pisky. He brought me. Anyway, he's part human."

Zennor said, "I am *here*, you know. Hello, Xavier. You got off the galleon without being savaged by the seafay, I see."

"Yes thanks. Not that they'd have any reason to savage me. I'm not a pisky."

Pip noted the slightly sticky atmosphere and recalled from her reading of *Leprechauns, Piskies, and Pixies* that elves and piskies didn't necessarily get along.

"Cut that out," she said. "I don't want to see you two posturing. I want to see my bucket."

The men stared one another down for five seconds and relaxed.

Zen gave Xavier a slap on the shoulder. "Good to see you, Xav. How's the very beautiful Nelis?"

"Very beautiful. How's the delightful Githa?"

"Delightful."

"Stop it with the double-act," Pip said.

They laughed. They were both around the same height and both had dark hair, but Xavier looked a few years older.

Probably not schoolmates, then.

Xavier indicated the crate again. "In there, Miss Pearmain. Check it over and make sure it comes up to expectations."

Pip pried up the lid and looked down into a crateful of shavings. She spotted a curved edge and grasped it. The handle came up, but the bucket it was attached to was unexpectedly heavy. Pip hoisted, but with her lack of height she was unable to get it even halfway to clearing of the brim of the crate.

Zennor bent to help her, lifting it out onto a patch of grass. It was enormous. Pip thought she could have got into it just as she was.

She stared at her new treasure with dawning delight.

Pretty she'd asked for, and *pretty* she'd got. Xavier had made her a sturdy wooden bucket with a neatly carved handle and a padded lid. "You can use it as a stool," he explained.

"I'd never be able to get up on it."

"You could always get a stepladder." Zen seemed disproportionately amused.

"It's not *that* high."

"Or a hassock," Xavier suggested.

"Hush, you." Pip went on with her inspection. The bucket was a rich honey colour with darker wooden eyes and a shimmering silken effect, reminding her of the wooden panelling she had seen in an old church. It was almost plain, but for a frieze of coloured carving below the rim. Pip plopped onto her knees to look more closely. Apples and roses and berries made wreathes in shades of red and gold with occasional green leaves.

Pip ran her fingers over the carvings. "It's *lovely*." The seat was pale straw coloured.

Xavier said, "Flowers and fruit always look good in carving. Open the lid."

Pip lifted the lid and laid it gently aside. She peered in and saw immediately why the bucket had been so heavy. Inside it nestled another bucket. Pip hoisted it out with help from Zen. This one was painted cream and carved all over with cats and horses, hounds and dolphins in naturalistic colours.

Pip felt like purring. "*Two* buckets!" She asked for one, and she supposed he'd charge her extra, but *two buckets!*

Xavier's rather serious face lit up in a smile. "Matryoshka buckets. You like them?"

Zen laughed and gave the elf man a gentle punch on the shoulder. "I'd say she liked them."

Xavier said, "Open the lid."

Pip opened the lid. Inside . . . She looked up, entranced. "However many are there?"

"Seven," Xavier said. "I know you asked for just one, but Nel pointed out you'd wanted a *functional* bucket and she said the first one is rather too big for someone . . . um . . ."

"As small and as old as me," Pip said. She lifted out bucket number three, which was painted pale green, and garlanded with cherry trees. A knight and his lady rode under the blossoming boughs.

Perfect.

The fourth was a forest bucket, with dark, mysterious trees.

"In case you feel like contemplating the inner darkness," Xavier said.

The fifth was painted with peacocks.

"Because everyone ought to have a peacock or eleven in their lives," Zen said drily.

The sixth was black. It sparkled with constellations that formed animals.

The seventh, approximately the size of the Lenten Rose bucket Pip had found in her crates at home, was painted in shades of blue with wispy clouds.

Pip opened that one to look at the inside and spotted something else. She lifted out a miniature Pippin Pearmain, wearing a pink dress and holding a matching bucket.

"I suppose technically it's eight buckets," Xavier said thoughtfully.

Pip looked in the miniature bucket and took out a child's-thimble-sized pot of marmalade.

"That's my logo," Xavier said. "You can wear it as a necklace. Or not."

Pip stared.

"My God, you've rendered the woman speechless," Zennor said. "I wouldn't have thought that was possible."

Neither had Pip.

She gloated for a full minute before she turned her attention back to the two fay men. They were different orders, but they managed to wear the same expressions when they regarded her.

"How did you two come to be friends?" she asked abruptly.

Zennor narrowed his eyes. "We're not."

"You are so," Pip insisted. She wasn't sure why she thought so, but she knew she was right. "You're alike," she added.

They shot her identical cranky looks.

"There!" She pointed a forefinger at each of them. "You're both tall and dark. You both love your wives. You stand the same way." She mirrored them. "You—" She indicated Xavier. "You made a cradle for *his* baby." She indicated Zen.

"He paid me," Xavier objected.

"He trusted you to make something for someone he loves. I bet it's a gorgeous cradle. Right?"

Xavier nodded slightly.

"Describe it."

"Honey-coloured wood, painted with cream and yellow roses," Zen said.

"There you are, then. And besides, you're both lurking at the end of the alphabet. You *ought* to be friends, so you are."

Zennor lifted one shoulder and turned to Xavier. "I think it's time we went."

"I have to pay the man first," Pip said, patting the largest bucket. She stood back as Xavier reassembled the matryoshka buckets into their nested form.

"Pay him, then. Shall I do the honours?"

"The — oh, yes. Will they fit?"

"They'll fit." Zen laid two fingers on the padded lid and the buckets vanished.

"Where are they?" Pip demanded.

"Cabin Six on the island."

"Okay. Grand." Pip hummed for a few seconds. "Do you take credit cards?" she asked Xavier.

"I do."

"Okay. What's the damage?"

"I gave you a quote."

"Yes. Might be less. Won't be more, you said. But that was for *one* bucket."

Xavier stuck his hands in his pockets. "I know, but Nel said — "

"Yes, that one was too big. But — "

"Just pay him what you agreed," Zennor said.

Pip's Mark One Pink Princess had never heard of internet banking, but Xavier produced a tablet that understood the system. Pip made the transaction without a qualm. If either of these two ever tried to misappropriate her funds, she'd butter the buckets and eat them.

Payment made, she said again, "So, how did you two come to be friends?"

Xavier said, "I was at school with Nel and Lucy."

Nel was his wife, but who the heck was Lucy?

Zennor nodded. "That's right." He turned to Pip. "There's a school called Diversity High where a lot of fay kids go. Soft integration. Xav and the very beautiful Nelis and an oddball called Lucy Tan were in the same year. Lucy's cousin is called Dequan Qin. Dequan had mislaid his girlfriend . . ."

"Tamzin," Pip supplied.

"The very same. So the three musketeers started pondering what might have happened to Tamzin, but before they got far with it, Tamzin walked into Dad's office — he's a solicitor.

Next thing, Dad brought her home to meet Ma and she moved in for a few weeks."

Pip frowned, trying to follow that. "Ja. *Und?*"

Xavier said, "*Und* nothing, really, but Lucy was *looking* for her, and Zennor's parents *had* her and eventually . . ." He laughed, unexpectedly. "I was at the gardens on the day of her wedding to Matin, but at the time I had no idea it was *her*. I just saw a lovely woman wearing a rainbow. And I knew Matin, obviously. So of course he got me to make the cradle."

"Why of course?"

"He's an elf," Zennor said.

Pip waited for enlightenment, but the men seemed to think that explained it.

"We'd better go," Zennor said to Xavier. He gave the elf man a pat on the shoulder. "See you around, Xav."

"Thank you," Pip said, beaming at the wood carver.

He put out a hand and she shook it. Then she turned and followed Zen back to the car.

"You're the same in another way, too," she remarked as he opened the door for her.

"Are you the kind of lady who likes to be helped into cars?" he asked.

"What do *you* think?"

"No."

"Right."

She got in and he did too.

"So?" Zen put the car in gear and pulled away from the Fairy Gardens.

So . . . Oh!

Pip settled herself and crossed her ankles. She felt entirely pleased with life. "You both wanted me to have what I wanted, and you made it happen," she said.

"Why wouldn't we?" Zen asked.

Pip closed her eyes. "No reason in the world, but you'd be

surprised at how many people *don't."*

Pip's story concludes in *Performing Pippin Pearmain 9*

ABOUT THE AUTHOR

Lark Westerly loves writing series where characters weave in and out of one another's stories.

She also loves playing with ideas and notions and researching odd information.

Lark lives in the island state of Tasmania, where she walks dogs, invents recipes, and goes around in clothes with that lived-in look. She rarely finds a matching pair of socks.

Unlike Pippin Pearmain, Lark is not tiny, not an only child, not single and not an on-screen performer. She never learned ballet and she can't speak Cat-Morse. She doesn't even have a bucket list. Nevertheless, Pippin Pearmain and Lark Westerly are sisters under the skin.

Oh . . . you were wondering about that bucket that inspired *Performing Pippin Pearmain*? It happened like this . . .

To find out, visit http://www.performingpippinpearmain.weebly.com and click on *About the Bucket List*.

www.ingramcontent.com/pod-product-compliance
Lightning Source LLC
Chambersburg PA
CBHW060630130626
46555CB00002B/739